"You indicated in your reservation that you weren't sure how long you'd want the room?" Rachel hoped for something a little more definite. In order to come out ahead financially, the inn needed a good holiday season.

"I don't know." Tyler shrugged. "I'm here to do something about my grandfather's property next door. My mother let it slide for too long."

It would be impolite to agree. "I'm sure the neighbors will be glad to help in any way they can. Are you planning to stay?"

"Live there, you mean?" His eyes narrowed. "Certainly not. I expect to sell as soon as possible."

"That's too bad. It would have been nice to hear that family would be living there again."

Now his look suggested that she'd lost her mind. "I'm hardly likely to want to live in the house where my grandfather was murdered."

Books by Marta Perry

Love Inspired Suspense

Love Inspired

MARTA PERRY

has written everything, including Sunday school curriculum, travel articles and magazine stories in twenty years of writing, but she feels she's found her home in the stories she writes for the Love Inspired line.

Marta lives in rural Pennsylvania, but she and her husband spend part of each year at their second home in South Carolina. When she's not writing, she's probably visiting her children and her five beautiful grandchildren, traveling or relaxing with a good book.

Marta loves hearing from readers, and she'll write back with a signed bookplate or bookmark. Write to her c/o Steeple Hill Books, 233 Broadway, Suite 1001, New York, NY 10279, e-mail her at marta@martaperry.com or visit her on the Web at www.martaperry.com.

A Christmas To Die For

Marta Perry

WWW.THRIFTYOWL.COM

Steeple
Hill®

Published by Steeple Hill Books™

STEEPLE HILL BOOKS

Steeple
Hill®

ISBN-13: 978-0-373-44265-2
ISBN-10:   0-373-44265-3

A CHRISTMAS TO DIE FOR

www.SteepleHill.com

Printed in U.S.A.

The salvation of the righteous comes from the Lord;
He is their stronghold in time of trouble. The Lord
helps them and delivers them; He delivers them
from the wicked and saves them, because
they take refuge in Him.

—*Psalms* 37:39–40

This story is dedicated to my supportive
and patient husband, Brian, with much love.

ONE

Rachel Hampton stood on the dark country road where, seven months ago, she'd nearly died. The dog pressed against her leg, shivering a little, either from the cold of the December evening or because he sensed her fear.

No, not fear. That would be ridiculous. It had been an accident, at least partially her fault for jogging along remote Crossings Road in the dark. She'd thought herself safe enough on the berm of the little-used gravel road, wearing a pale jacket with reflective stripes that should have been apparent to any driver.

Obviously it hadn't been. He'd come around the bend too fast, his lights blinding her when she'd glanced over her shoulder. But now she was over it, she—

Her heart pumped into overdrive. The roar of a motor, lights reflected from the trees. A car was coming. He wouldn't see her. She'd be hit again, thrown into the air, helpless—

She grabbed Barney's collar and stumbled back into the pines, pulse pounding, a sob catching in her throat as she fought to control the panic.

But the car was slowing, stopping. The driver's-side window slid smoothly down.

"Excuse me." A male voice, deep and assured. "Can you tell me how to get to Three Sisters Inn?"

How nice of him to ignore the fact that she'd leaped into the bushes when she heard him coming. She disentangled her hair from the long needles of a white pine and moved toward him.

"You've missed the driveway," she said. "This is a back road that just leads to a few isolated farms." She approached the car with Barney, Grams's sheltie, close by her side. "If you back up a bit, you can turn into a farm lane that will take you to the inn parking lot."

He switched on the dome light, probably to reassure her. Black hair and frowning brows over eyes that were a deep, deep blue, a pale-gray sweater over a dress shirt and dark tie, a glint of gold from the watch on his wrist, just visible where his hand rested on the steering wheel. He didn't look like a tourist, come to gawk at the Amish farmers or buy a handmade quilt. The briefcase and laptop that rested on the passenger seat indicated that.

"You're sure the proprietor won't mind my coming in that way?"

She smiled. "The proprietor would be me, and I don't mind at all. I'm Rachel Hampton. You must be Mr. Dunn." Since she and Grams expected only one visitor, that wasn't hard to figure out.

"Tyler Dunn. Do you want a lift?"

"Thanks, but it's not far. Besides, I have the dog." And I don't get into a car with a stranger, even if he does have a reservation at the inn.

Maybe it was her having come so close to death that had blunted her carefree ways. Either that or the responsibility of starting the bed-and-breakfast on a shoestring had forced her to grow up. No more drifting from job to job, taking on a new restaurant each time she became bored. She was settled now, and it was up to her to make a success of this.

She stepped back, still holding Barney's collar despite his wiggling, and waited until the car pulled into the lane before following it to the shortcut. She'd walked down the main road, the way the car had come, but this was faster. She gestured Dunn to a parking space in the gravel pull-off near the side door to the inn.

He stepped out, shrugging into a leather jacket, and stood looking up at the inn. It was well worth looking at, even on a cold December night. Yellow light gleamed from the candles they'd placed in every one of the many nine-paned windows. Security lights posted on the outbuildings cast a pale-golden glow over the historic Federal-style sandstone mansion. It had been home to generations of the Unger family before necessity had turned it into the Three Sisters Inn.

Rachel glanced at the man, expecting him to say something. Guests usually sounded awed or at least admiring, at first sight. Dunn just turned to haul his briefcase and computer from the front seat.

Definitely not the typical tourist. What had brought him to the heart of Pennsylvania Dutch country at this time of year? Visiting businessmen, especially those who traveled alone, were more likely to seek out a hotel with wireless connection and fax machines rather than a bed-and-breakfast, no matter how charming.

"May I carry something for you?"

He handed her the computer case. "If you'll take this, I can manage the rest."

The case was heavier than she'd expected, and she straightened, determined not to give in to the limp that sometimes plagued her when she was tired—the only remaining souvenir of the accident.

Or at least she'd thought that was the only after-effect, until she'd felt that surge of terror when she'd seen the car. She'd have to work on that.

"This way. We'll go in the side door instead of around to the front, if you don't mind."

"Fine."

A man of few words, apparently. Dog at her heels, she headed for the door, hearing his footsteps behind her. She glanced back. He was taller than she'd realized when he sat in the car—he probably had a good foot on her measly five two, and he moved with a long stride that had him practically on her heels.

She went into the hallway, welcoming the flow of warm air, and on into the library. She didn't usually bring guests in through the family quarters, but it seemed silly to walk around the building just to give him the effect of the imposing front entrance into the high-ceiled center hall. The usual visitor ohhed and ahhed over that. She had a feeling Tyler Dunn wouldn't.

"My grandmother has already gone up to bed." She led the way to the desk. "You'll meet her in the morning at breakfast. We serve from seven-thirty to nine-thirty, but you can make arrangements to have it earlier, if you wish."

He shook his head, glancing toward the glowing embers of the fire she'd started earlier. Grams's favorite chair was drawn up next to the fireplace, and her knitting lay on its arm.

"That's fine. If I can just get signed in now and see my room—"

"Of course." Smile, she reminded herself. The customer is always right. She handed him a registration card and a pen, stepping back so that he had room to fill it out.

He bent over, printing the information in quick, black strokes, frowning a little. He looked tired and drawn, she realized, her quick sympathy stirring.

"That's great, thanks." She imprinted the credit card and handed it back to him. "You indicated in your reservation that you weren't sure how long you'd want the room?"

She made it a question, hoping for something a little more definite. With all the work she'd been doing to lure guests for the holiday season, the inn still wasn't booked fully. January and February were bound to be quiet. In order to come out ahead financially, they needed a good holiday season. Her money worries seemed to pop up automatically several times a day.

"I don't know." He almost snapped the words. She must have shown a reaction, because almost immediately he gave her a slightly rueful smile. "Sorry. I hope that doesn't inconvenience you, but I have business in the area, and I don't know how long it will take."

"Not at all." The longer she could rent him the room, the better. "Perhaps while you're here, you'll have time to enjoy some of the Christmas festivities. The village is planning a number of events, and of course we're not far from Bethlehem—"

"I'm not here for sightseeing." His gaze was on the dying fire, not her, but she seemed to sense him weighing a decision to say more. "That business I spoke of—there's no reason you'd recognize my name, but I own the property that adjoins yours on one side. The old Hostetler farm."

She blinked. "I didn't realize—" She stopped, not sure how to phrase the question. "I thought the property belonged to John Hostetler's daughter."

Who had annoyed the neighbors by refusing to sell the property and neglecting to take proper care of it. The farmhouse and barn had been invaded by vandals more than once, and the thrifty Amish farmers who owned the adjoining land been offended at the sight of a good farm going to ruin.

"My mother," he said shortly. His face drew a bit tighter. "She died recently."

That went a long way toward explaining the tension she felt from him. It didn't excuse his curtness, but made it more understandable. He was still grieving his mother's death and was now forced to deal with the unfinished business she'd left behind.

"I'm so sorry." She reached out impulsively to touch his arm. "You have my sympathy."

He jerked a nod. "I'm here to do something about my grandfather's property. My mother let that slide for too long."

It would be impolite to agree. "I'm sure the neighbors will be glad to help in any way they can. Are you planning to stay?"

"Live there, you mean?" His eyes narrowed. "Certainly not. I expect to sell as soon as possible."

Something new to worry about, as if she didn't have enough already. The best offer for the Hostetler farm might easily come from someone who wanted to put up some obnoxious faux Amish atrocity within sight of the inn.

"That's too bad. It would have been nice to hear that family would be living there again."

She'd made the comment almost at random, but Tyler Dunn's expression suggested that she'd lost her mind.

"I don't know why you'd think that." He bit off the words. "I'm hardly likely to want to live in the house where my grandfather was murdered."

Tyler closed his laptop and glanced at his watch. A little after eight—time for breakfast and another encounter with the Unger family.

He stood, pushing the ladder-back chair away from the small table, which was the only spot in the bedroom where one could possibly use a computer. He must be the first person who'd checked into the Three Sisters Inn for business purposes. Most of the guests would be here to enjoy staying in the elegant mansion, maybe pretending they were living a century ago.

The place looked as if it belonged in a magazine devoted to historic homes. The bedroom, with its canopy bed covered by what was probably an Amish quilt, its antique furniture and deep casement windows, would look right on the cover.

From the window in his room, he had a good view of Churchville's Main Street, which was actually a country route along which the village had been built. The inn anchored the eastern edge of the community, along with the stone church which stood enclosed in its walled churchyard across the street. Beyond, there was nothing but hedgerows and the patchwork pattern of plowed fields and pasture, with barns and silos in the distance.

Looking to the left, he could see the shops and restaurants along Main Street, more than he'd expect given the few blocks of residential properties, but probably the flood of tourism going through town accounted for that. The inn had a desirable position, almost in the country but within easy walking distance of Main Street attractions. It was surprising they weren't busier.

He opened the door. The upstairs landing was quiet, the doors to the other rooms standing open. Obviously, he was the only guest at the moment. Maybe that would make things easier.

Had it been a mistake to come out so bluntly with the fact of his grandfather's murder last night? He wasn't sure, and he didn't like not being sure. He was used to dealing with facts, figures, formulas—not something as amorphous as this.

At least he'd had an opportunity to see Rachel Hampton's reaction. He frowned. Her name might be Hampton, but she was one of the Unger family.

If his mother had been right—but he couldn't count on that. In any event, he'd understood what she'd wanted of him. The impossible.

He started down the staircase, running his hand along the delicately carved railing. The downstairs hall stretched from front to back of the house. To his right, the door into the library where he'd registered last night was now closed. On his left, a handsome front parlor opened into another parlor, slightly smaller, behind it, both decorated with period furniture.

He headed toward the rear of the building, where Rachel had indicated he'd find the breakfast room. He'd cleared his calendar until the first of the year. If he couldn't accomplish what he planned by then, he'd put his grandfather's farm on the market, go back to his own life and try to forget.

The hallway opened out into a large, rectangular sunroom, obviously an addition to the original house. A wall of windows looked onto a patio and garden, bare of flowers now, but still worth looking at in the shapes of the trees and the bright berries of the shrubs. The long table was set for one.

Voices came from the doorway to the left, obviously the kitchen. He moved quietly toward them.

"…if I'd known, maybe I wouldn't have opened my mouth and put my foot in it." Rachel, obviously talking to someone about his arrival.

"There was no reason for you to know. You were just a child." An older voice, cultured, restrained. If this woman was hiding something, he couldn't tell.

A pan clattered. "You'd best see if he's coming down, before these sticky buns are cold."

That was his cue, obviously. He moved to the doorway before someone could come out and find him. "I'm here. I wouldn't want to cause a crisis in the kitchen."

"Good morning." The woman who rose from the kitchen table, extending her hand to him, must be Rachel's grandmother. Every bit the grande dame, she didn't look in the least bothered by what he might or might not have overheard. "Welcome to the inn, Mr. Dunn. I'm Katherine Unger."

"Thank you." He shook her hand gently, aware of bones as fine as delicate crystal. The high cheekbones, brilliant blue eyes, and assured carriage might have belonged to a duchess.

Rachel, holding a casserole dish between two oversize oven mitts, had more color in her cheeks than he'd seen the night before, but maybe that was from the heat of the stove.

The third person in the kitchen wore the full-skirted dark dress and apron and white cap of the Amish. She turned away, evading his gaze, perhaps shy of a stranger.

"It's a pleasure to meet you, Mrs. Unger. I suppose your granddaughter told you who I am."

"Yes. I was very sorry to hear of your mother's death. I knew her when she was a girl, although I don't suppose she remembered me. I don't remember seeing her again after she graduated from high school."

"Actually, she spoke of you when she talked about her childhood." Which hadn't been often, for the most part, until her final days. He'd always thought she'd been eager to forget.

"I'm sure you'd like to have your breakfast. Rachel has fixed her wild-mushroom and sausage quiche for you."

"You can have something else, if you prefer," Rachel said quickly. "I didn't have a chance to ask—"

"It sounds great," he said. "And I'm looking forward to the sticky buns, too." He smiled in the direction of the Amish woman, but she stared down at the stovetop as if it might speak to her.

Rachel, carrying the steaming casserole dish, led the way to the table in the breakfast room. He sat down, but before he had a chance to say anything, she'd whisked off to the kitchen, to reappear in a moment with a basket of rolls.

He helped himself to a fresh fruit cup and smiled at her as she poured coffee. "Any chance you'd pour a cup and join me? It's a little strange sitting here by myself."

This time there was no mistaking the flush that colored her cheeks. That fair skin must make it hard to camouflage her feelings. "I'm sorry there aren't any other guests at the moment, but—"

"Please. I need to apologize, and it would be easier over coffee."

She gave him a startled look, then turned without a

word and took a mug from a mammoth china cupboard that bore faded stenciling—apples, tulips, stars. It stood against the stone wall that must once have been the exterior of the house.

Her mug filled, she sat down opposite him. "There's really no reason for you to apologize to me."

Green eyes serious in a heart-shaped face, brown hair curling to the shoulders of the white shirt she wore with jeans, her hands clasped around the mug—she looked about sixteen instead of the twenty-nine he knew her to be. He'd done his homework on the residents of Three Sisters Inn before he'd come.

"I think I do. You were being friendly, and I shouldn't have thrown the fact of my grandfather's death at you."

"I didn't know." Her eyes were troubled, he'd guess because she was someone who hated hurting another's feelings. "We left here when I was about eight, and I didn't come back until less than a year ago, so I'm not up on local history."

"I guess that's what it seems like." He tried to pull up his own images of his grandfather, but it was too long ago. "Ancient history. I remember coming for the funeral and having the odd sense that conversations broke off when I came in the room. It must have been years before I knew my grandfather had been killed in the course of a robbery."

She leaned toward him, sympathy in every line of her body. "I'm sure it's hard to deal with things so soon after your mother's death. Is there any other family to help you?"

"I'm afraid not." He found himself responding to her warmth even while the analytical part of his mind registered that the way to gain her cooperation was to need her help. "I hate the thought of seeing the farm again after all this time. It's down that road I was on last night, isn't it?"

He paused, waiting for the offer he was sure she'd feel compelled to make.

Rachel's fingers clenched around the mug, and he could sense the reluctance in her. And see her overcome it.

"Would you like me to go over there with you?"

"You'd do that?"

She smiled, seeming to overcome whatever reservation she had. "Of course. We're neighbors, after all."

It took a second to adjust to the warmth of that smile. "Thanks. I'd appreciate it."

Careful. He took a mental step back. Rachel Hampton was a very attractive woman, but he couldn't afford to be distracted from the task that had brought him here. And if she knew, there might very well be no more offers of help.

The dog danced at Rachel's heels as she walked down Crossings Road beside Tyler that afternoon. At least Barney was excited about this outing. She was beginning to regret that impulsive offer to accompany Tyler. And as for him—well, he looked as if every step brought him closer to something he didn't want to face.

Fanciful, she scolded herself, shoving her hands into the pockets of her corduroy jacket. The sun was bright enough to make her wish she'd brought sunglasses, but the air was crisp and cold.

"There's the lane to the farmhouse." She pointed ahead to the wooden gate that sagged between two posts. If there'd ever been a fence along the neglected pasture, it was long gone. "Is it coming back to you at all?"

Tyler shook his head. "I only visited my grandfather once before the time I came for the funeral. Apparently, he and my mother didn't get along well."

From what Grams had told her this morning, John Hostetler hadn't been on friendly terms with anybody, but it would hardly be polite to tell Tyler that. "That's a shame. This was a great place to be a kid."

Her gesture took in the gently rolling farmland that stretched in every direction, marked into neat fields, some sere and brown after the harvest, others showing the green haze of winter wheat.

He followed her movement, narrowing his eyes against the sun. "Are those farms Amish?"

"All the ones you see from here are. The Zook farm is the closest—we share a boundary with them, and you must, as well." She pointed. "Over there are the Stolzfuses, then the Bredbenners, and that farthest one belongs to Jacob Stoker. Amish farms may be different in other places, but around here you'll usually see a white bank barn and two silos. You won't see electric lines."

He gave her an amused look. "You sound like the local tour guide."

"Sorry. I guess it comes with running a B&B."

He looked down the lane at the farmhouse, just coming into view. "There it is. I can't say it brings any nostalgic feeling. My grandfather didn't seem welcoming when we came here. If my mother ever wanted to change things with him—well, I guess she left it too late."

Was he thinking again about his grandfather's funeral? Or maybe regretting the relationship they'd never had? She knew a bit about that feeling. Her father had never spent enough time in her life to do anything but leave a hole.

"You said something this morning about conversations breaking off when you came in the room—people wanting to protect you, I suppose, from knowing how your grandfather died."

He nodded, a question in his eyes.

"I know how that feels. When my father walked out, no one would tell us anything." She shook her head, almost wishing she hadn't spoken. After all these years, she still didn't like thinking about it. But that was what made her understand how Tyler felt. "Maybe they figured because he'd never been around much anyway, we wouldn't realize that this time was for good, but the truth would have been better than what we imagined."

His deep-blue eyes were so intent on her face that it was almost as if he touched her. "That must have been rough on you and your sisters."

She registered his words with a faint sense of unease. "I don't believe I mentioned my sisters to you."

"Didn't you?" He smiled, but there was something guarded in the look. "I suppose I was making an assumption, because of the inn's name."

That was logical, although it didn't entirely take away her startled sense that he knew more about them than she'd expect from a casual visitor.

"The name may be wishful thinking on my part, but yes, I have two sisters. Andrea is the oldest. She was married at Thanksgiving, and she and her husband are still on a honeymoon trip. And Caroline, the youngest, is an artist, living out in Santa Fe." She touched the turquoise and silver pin on her shirt collar. "She made this."

Tyler stopped, bending to look at the delicate hummingbird. He was so close his fingers almost touched her neck as he straightened the collar, and she was suddenly warm in spite of the chill breeze.

He drew back, and the momentary awareness was gone. "It's lovely. Your sister is talented."

"Yes." The worry over Caro that lurked at the back of her mind surfaced. Something had been wrong when Caro came home for the wedding, hidden behind her too-brittle laugh and almost frantic energy. But Caroline didn't seem to need her sisters any longer.

"The place looks even worse than I expected." Tyler's words brought her back to the present. The farmhouse, a simple frame building with a stone chimney at either end, seemed to sag as if tired of trying to stand upright. The porch that extended across the front sported broken railings and crumbling steps, and several windows had been boarded up.

"Grams told me the house had been broken into several times. Some of the neighbors came and boarded up the windows after the last incident. The barn looks in fairly good shape, though."

That was a small consolation to hold out to him if he really hadn't known that his mother let the place fall to bits. Still, a good solid Pennsylvania Dutch bank barn could withstand almost anything except fire.

"If those hex signs were meant to protect the place, they're not doing a very good job." He was looking up at the peak of the roof, where a round hex sign with the familiar star pattern hung.

"I don't think you'd find anyone to admit they believe that. Most people just say they're a tradition. There are as many theories as there are scholars who study them."

Tyler went cautiously up the porch steps and then turned toward her. "You'll have to climb over the broken tread."

She grasped the hand he held out, and he almost lifted her to the porch. She whistled to the dog, nosing around the base of the porch. "Come, Barney. The last thing we need is for you to unearth a hibernating skunk."

"That would be messy." Tyler turned a key in the lock, and the door creaked open. He hesitated for an instant and then stepped inside. She followed, switching on the flashlight that Grams had reminded her to bring.

"Dusty." A little light filtered through the boards on the windows, and the beam of her flashlight danced around the room, showing a few remaining pieces of furniture, a massive stone fireplace on the end wall, and a thick layer of dust on everything.

Tyler stood in the middle of the room, very still. His face seemed stiff, almost frozen.

"I'm sorry if it's a disappointment. It was a good,

sturdy farmhouse once, and it could be again, with some money and effort."

"I doubt I'd find anyone interested in doing that." He walked through the dining room toward the kitchen, and she followed him, trying to think of something encouraging to say. This had to be a sad homecoming for him.

"There's an old stone sink. You don't often see those in their original state anymore."

He sent her the ghost of a smile. "You want to try out the pump?"

"No, thanks. That looks beyond repair. But I can imagine some antique dealer drooling over the stone sink. Those are quite popular now."

"I suppose I should get a dealer out to see if there's anything worth selling. I remember the house as being crowded with furniture, but there's not too much left now."

"My grandmother could steer you to some reputable dealers. Didn't your mother take anything back with her after your grandfather died?"

She couldn't help being curious. Anyone would be. Why had the woman let the place fall apart after her father died? Grief, maybe, but it still seemed odd. Surely she knew how valuable a good farm was in Lancaster County.

"Not that I remember." He turned from a contemplation of the cobwebby ice box to focus on her. "You spoke of break-ins. Was anything stolen?"

"I don't know. My grandmother might remember. Or Emma Zook, since they're such close neighbors. She's our housekeeper."

"The Amish woman who was in the kitchen this morning? According to the lawyer who handled my grandfather's will, the Zooks leased some of the farmland from his estate. I need to get that straightened out before I put the place on the market. I should talk to them. And to your grandmother."

Something about his intent look made her uneasy. "I doubt that she knows anything about their leases."

"According to my mother, Fredrick Unger offered to buy the property. That would make me think your family had an interest."

There was something—an edgy, almost antagonistic tone to his voice, that set her back up instantly. What was he driving at?

"I'm sure my grandfather's only interest would have been to keep a valuable farm from falling to pieces. Since he died nearly five years ago, I don't imagine you'll ever know."

"Your grandmother—"

"My grandmother was never involved in his business interests." And she wasn't going to allow him to badger her with questions. "I can't see that it matters, since your mother obviously didn't want to sell. Maybe what you need to do is talk to the attorney."

Her own tone was as sharp as his had been. She wasn't sure where the sudden tension had come from, but it was there between them. She could feel it, fierce and insistent.

Tyler's frown darkened, but before he could speak, there was a noisy creak from the living room.

"Hello? Anybody here?"

"Be right there," she called. She'd never been quite so pleased to hear Phillip Longstreet's voice. She didn't know where Tyler had been going with his questions and his attitude, and she didn't think she wanted to.

TWO

Tyler didn't miss the relief on Rachel's face at the interruption. The speed with which she went into the living room was another giveaway. She might not know what drove him, but she'd picked up on something.

Or else he'd been careless, pushing too hard in his drive to get this situation resolved.

He followed her and found her greeting the newcomer with some surprise. "Phillip. What are you doing here?"

The man raised his eyebrows as she evaded his attempt to hug her. "Aren't you going to introduce me?" He held out his hand to Tyler. "Phillip Longstreet. You may have noticed Longstreet Antiques on Main Street in the village."

He was in his late forties or early fifties at a guess, but he wore his age well—fit-looking, with fair hair that showed signs of gray at the temples and shrewd hazel eyes behind the latest style in glasses.

"This is Tyler Dunn." She glanced at him, and he thought he read a warning in her eyes.

"Nice to meet you. Were you looking for Ms. Hampton?"

"It's always pleasant to see Rachel, but no, I wanted to meet the new owner." Longstreet shrugged, smiling. "I like to get in before the other dealers when I can."

"How did you know?" Rachel sounded exasperated. "If we had a party line, Phillip, I'd suspect you of eavesdropping."

"I have to be far more creative than that to stay ahead of the competition. If you want to keep secrets, don't come to a village. Emma's son, Levi, delivered the news along with my eggs this morning."

It was an insight into how this place worked. "Are you interested in the contents of the house, Mr. Longstreet?"

A local dealer might be the best choice before putting the house on the market, but Longstreet was obviously trolling for antiques, probably hoping to get an offer in on anything of value before his competition did. Or possibly before Tyler realized what he had.

"Phil, please. I'd like to look around." Longstreet's gaze was already scoping out the few pieces left in the living room. "Sometimes there are attractive pieces in these old farmhouses, although more often it's a waste of time."

"I'm afraid your time was definitely wasted this afternoon." He gestured toward the door. "I'm not ready to make a decision about selling anything yet."

"If I could just take a look around, I might be able to give you an idea of values." Longstreet craned his neck toward the dining room.

Tyler swung the door open and stepped out onto the porch, so that the man had no choice but to follow. "I'll be in touch when I'm ready to make a decision. Thank you for stopping by."

"Yes, well, thanks for your time." Longstreet stepped gingerly over the broken step. "Rachel, I'll see you at the meeting tonight."

Rachel, coming out behind him, bent to snap a leash onto the dog's collar. "Fine."

Tyler waited until Longstreet had backed out of the driveway to turn to her. "Is that one of the reputable dealers your grandmother might recommend?"

"Grams probably *would* suggest him. His uncle was an old crony of my grandfather."

"But…?"

Her nose crinkled. "Phil's nice enough, in his way. It's just that every time he comes to the inn, I get the feeling he's putting a price on the furniture."

"I'm not bad at showing people the door, if you'd like some help."

"I run an inn, remember?" She smiled, her earlier antagonism apparently gone. "The idea is to get people in, not send them away. Are you a bouncer in your real life?"

"Architect. Showing people the way out is just a sideline."

She looked interested. "Do you work on your own?"

He shook his head. "I'm with a partner in Baltimore, primarily designing churches and public buildings. Luckily I'm between projects right now, so I can take some time off to deal with this." Which brought him back to the problem at hand. "Well, if your grandmother recommends Longstreet, I'll still be sure to get offers from more than one dealer."

"That should keep him in line. He's probably easier to cope with when he wants to buy something from you. I'm on the Christmas in Churchville committee with him, and he can be a real pain there."

He pulled the door shut and turned the key in the lock.

"Are you sure you're finished? You didn't look around upstairs."

"I've had enough for the moment." He tried to dismiss the negative feelings that had come with seeing the place again. This was a fool's errand. There was no truth left to find here—just a moldering ruin that had never, as far as he could tell, been a happy home.

The dog leaped down from the porch, nearly pulling Rachel off balance, and he caught her arm to steady her.

"Easy. Does he really need to be on the leash?"

"I wanted to discourage any more digging around the porch. I'm afraid you may have something holed up in there for the winter."

"Whatever it is, let it stay." He took the leash from her hand and helped her over the broken step to the ground. "I won't bother it."

She glanced at him as they walked away. "You must be saddened to see the place in such a state."

He shrugged. "I only saw it twice that I recall. It would have been worse for my mother than for me. She grew up here."

"Do you think—" She stopped, as if censoring what she'd been about to say.

"That's why she let it fall to pieces?" He finished the thought for her. "I have no idea. I'd have expected my dad to intercede, but—" he shrugged "—I didn't know she still owned the place until a few weeks ago, and by then she was in no shape to explain much. Maybe she just wanted to forget, after the way her father died."

Rachel scuffed through frost-tipped dead leaves that the wind had scattered over the road. "I don't think I've ever actually heard how it happened."

"From what my mother told me, he apparently confronted someone breaking into the house. There was a struggle, and he had a heart attack. He wasn't found until the next day."

She shivered, shoving her hands into her pockets. "It's hard to think about something like that happening here when I was a child. It always seemed such an idyllic place."

They walked for a few moments in silence, their footsteps muted on the macadam road. He glanced at her, confirming what he heard. "You're limping. Did you twist your ankle getting off that porch?"

"It wasn't that." She nodded toward the bend in the road ahead of them, the wind ruffling her hair across her face so that she pushed it back with an impatient movement. "I had an accident just up the road back in the spring."

He frowned down at her. "It must have been a bad one. Did you hit a tree?"

She shook her head. "I was jogging, too late in the evening, I guess. A car came around the bend—" She stopped, probably reliving it too acutely.

That explained why she'd stepped back into the trees when he'd come down the lane last night. "How badly were you hurt?"

"Two broken legs." She shrugged. "Could have been worse, I guess. It only bothers me when I'm on my feet too long."

"I hope the driver ended up in jail."

"Hit and run," she said briefly.

Obviously she didn't want to talk about it any further. He couldn't blame her. She didn't want to remember, any more than he wanted to think about the way his grandfather died, or the burden his mother had laid on him to find out why.

"I guess this place isn't so idyllic after all."

"Bad things happen anywhere, people being people."

"Yes, I guess they do." Of course she was right about that. It was only the beauty that surrounded them that made violence seem so out of place here.

Rachel was thankful when the business part of the "Christmas in Churchville" meeting was over. The strain of mediating all those clashing egos had begun to tell on her after the first hour.

Now the battling committee members wandered around the public rooms of the inn, helping themselves to punch and the variety of goodies placed on tables in both the back parlor and the breakfast room.

She'd figured out a long time ago that if you wanted to keep people circulating, you should space out the food and drink.

She and Grams had put cranberry punch on the round table next to the fireplace in the back parlor, accompanied by an assortment of cheeses, grapes and crackers. The breakfast room had coffee, tea and hot chocolate on the sideboard, along with mini éclairs and pfeffernüsse, the tiny clove and cardamom delicacies that were her grandmother's special holiday recipe.

Would Tyler come down? Thinking of him alone in his room, she'd suggested he join them for refreshments. He'd know when the business meeting was over, she'd told him, when the shouting stopped.

Her committee members weren't quite that bad, but they did have strong opinions on what would draw the holiday tourists to spend their money in Churchville.

She checked on the service in the parlor and walked back toward the breakfast room. Tyler was in an odd position here—part of the community by heritage and yet a stranger. He probably wouldn't be around long enough to change that. He'd sell the property and go back to his life in Baltimore.

Hopefully he wouldn't leave problems behind in the form of whoever bought his grandfather's farm. The neighbors disliked seeing it derelict, but there were certainly things they'd hate even more.

"Rachel, there you are." Phillip intercepted her in the doorway, punch cup in hand. Fortunately the cup made it easier to escape the arm he tried to put around her. "I wanted to speak with you about the Hostetler place."

"So does everyone else, but I don't know anything. Tyler hasn't told me what his plans are for the property."

"You know I'm all about the furniture, my dear. I remember a dough box that my uncle tried to buy once from old Hostetler. If there's anything like that left—"

"You saw the living room. Most of the furniture is already gone."

"I didn't see the rest of the house." His voice turned wheedling. "Come on, Rachel, at least give me a hint what's there."

"Sorry, I didn't see anything else." She slipped past him. "Excuse me, but I have to refill the coffeepot."

Phillip was nothing if not persistent. That probably explained how he managed to make such a success of the shop. His uncle had been a sweet old man, but he'd never had much of a head for business, from what Grams said.

She snagged a mug of hot chocolate and a pfeffernüsse for herself, turning from the table to find Sandra Whitmoyer bearing down on her. As wife of Churchville's most dedicated, as well as only, physician, Sandra seemed to feel the chairmanship of the decorating subcommittee was hers by right. Luckily no one else had put up a fight for it.

"Rachel, we really must keep our eyes on the rest of the shop owners along Main Street. It would be fatal to allow anyone to put up a garish display."

"I'm sure you'll do a wonderful job of that, Sandra." She had no desire to turn herself into the decorating police. "I have my hands full already, preparing the inn and organizing the open house tour." Maybe a little flattery was in order. "You have such wonderful taste.

I know everyone will be seeking your advice. And they've all agreed to go along with the committee's decisions."

"Well, I suppose." Sandra ran a manicured hand over sleek waves of blond hair. She was dressed to perfection tonight as always, this time in a pair of gray wool slacks that made her legs look a mile long, paired with a silk shirt that had probably cost the earth.

Glancing past Sandra, she spotted Tyler standing in the doorway. So he had come down. He looked perfectly composed in the crowd of strangers—self-possessed, as if he carried his confidence with him no matter where he was.

She'd seen him ruffled at moments that afternoon, though, and she'd guess he didn't often show that side to people. The derelict house had affected him more than she'd expected.

And there had been an undercurrent when he talked about his mother, something more than grief, she thought.

Sandra had moved to the window, peering out at the patio and garden. "I suppose you'll be decorating the garden for the open house."

"White lights on the trees, and possibly colored ones on the big spruce."

"It would be more effective without the security lights," Sandra said. "You could turn them off during the house tour hours. And maybe put a spotlight on the gazebo."

"I don't want to draw attention to the gazebo. I'd be happy to demolish it completely."

"You wouldn't have to do something that drastic."

She turned at the sound of Tyler's voice, smiling her welcome. "What would you suggest, other than a stick of dynamite? Sandra Whitmoyer, I'd like to introduce Tyler Dunn. He owns the Hostetler place, down the road from us."

Sandra extended her hand. "Welcome to Church-ville. Everyone is curious about what you intend for the property. Well, not my husband, of course. As a busy physician, he doesn't have time for many outside interests."

Bradley Whitmoyer was as self-effacing a man as she'd ever met, but his wife had appointed herself his one-woman press agency.

Tyler responded, politely noncommittal, and turned back to Rachel. "I wouldn't recommend high explosives for the gazebo. You wouldn't like the results."

"I don't like it the way it is."

He smiled down at her. "That's because it's in the wrong place. If you moved it to the other side of the pond, it would be far enough away to create a view."

"Well, I still think you should decorate it for the house tour." Sandra put down her cup. "I have to go. There's Jeff looking for me. It was nice meeting you, Mr. Dunn." She nodded to Rachel and crossed the room toward the hallway.

"Is that her husband, the physician?" Tyler's tone was faintly mocking.

"No, his brother. Jeff Whitmoyer. He has a small construction company. It looks as if he didn't find it necessary to change before coming by for Sandra."

Jeff's blue jeans, flannel shirt and work boots were a sharp contrast to Sandra's elegance. There was a quick exchange between them before Sandra swept out the hallway.

Rachel dismissed them from her mind and turned back to Tyler. "About the gazebo—"

"Single-minded, aren't you?" His smile took any edge off the comment. "It might be possible to move it, rather than destroy it. If you like, I'll take a look while I'm here."

"I'd love to find a solution that makes everyone happy. Grams never liked the gazebo at all—she feels it doesn't go with the style of the house. But Andrea thinks it should stay because Grandfather had it put up as a surprise for Grams."

"And it's your job to keep everyone happy?" The corners of his mouth quirked.

"Not my job, exactly." Every family had a peace-maker, didn't they? She was the middle one, so it fell to her. "My sister says I let my nurturing instincts run amok, always trying to help people whether they want it or not."

"It's a nice quality." Those deep-blue eyes seemed to warm when they rested on her. "I wouldn't change if I were you."

"Thank you." Ridiculous, to be suddenly breathless because a man was looking at her with approval. "And thank you for the offer."

He shrugged. "It's nothing. We're neighbors, re-member?"

It was what she'd said to him, but he seemed to invest the words with a warmth that startled her.

Careful, she warned herself. It wouldn't be a good idea to start getting too interested in a man who'd disappear as soon as his business here was wound up.

Rachel did not like climbing ladders. Any ladder, let alone this mammoth thing that allowed her to reach the top of the house. Unfortunately, there didn't seem to be another way of putting up the outside lights anytime soon.

Grams had suggested hiring someone to do the decorating, but Grams didn't have a grasp on how tight money was right now. Rachel could ask a neighbor for help, of course, but this was a business. It didn't seem right if she couldn't pay.

But she really didn't like being up on a ladder.

She leaned out, bracing herself with one hand on the shutter, and slipped the strand of lights over the final hook. Breathing a sigh of relief, she went down the ladder. In comparison to that, doing the windows should be a breeze.

Reaching the ground, she took a step back, reminding herself of just how many windows there were. Well, maybe not a breeze, but she could do it.

And what difference would it make, the voice of doubt asked. You have one whole guest at the moment.

Tyler had gone off to Lancaster this morning to see the attorney who'd handled his grandfather's estate. He'd seemed eager to resolve the situation with the farm. Well, why not? He probably had plans for Christmas in Baltimore.

Once he left, she'd have zero guests. There were a

few people scheduled for the coming weekends, but not nearly enough. They'd hoped for a good holiday season to get them through the rest of the winter, but that wasn't happening.

If she could get some holiday publicity up on the inn's Web site, it might make all the difference. Andrea had intended to do that, but the rush to get ready for the wedding had swamped those plans. And she could hardly call her big sister on her honeymoon to ask for help. They had already invested all they could afford in print ads in the tourist guides, and the Web site was the only option left.

She fastened a spray of pine in place, taking satisfaction in the way the dark green contrasted with the pale stone walls. This she could do. Decorate, cook gourmet breakfasts, work twenty-four/seven when it was necessary—those were her gifts.

Her gaze rested absently on the church across the street, its stone walls as gold as the inn. Someone had put evergreen wreaths on the double doors, and the church glowed with welcome. That was what she'd sensed when she'd come back to Churchville. Welcome. Home. Family. Community. She'd lost that when Daddy left and their mother had taken them away from here.

She paused with her hand on the burgundy ribbon she was tying. *Lord, this venture can't be wrong, can it? It seems right. Surely You wouldn't let me have a need so strong if it weren't meant to be satisfied.*

"Rachel, you look as if you've turned to stone up there. Are you all right?"

She glanced down from the window to see Bradley Whitmoyer standing on the walk, eyeing her quizzically. She scrambled down from the stepladder.

"I guess that's what they mean by being lost in thought, Dr. Whitmoyer. What can I do for you?"

She saw him occasionally, of course, when she took Grams for a check-up, at church, at a social event, but he'd never come to the inn.

"Bradley," he corrected. "I'm on an errand." He gave her his gentle smile, pulling an envelope from the pocket of his overcoat. "My wife asked me to drop this off on my way to the office. Something to do with this Christmas celebration you're working on, I think."

She took the envelope. "You shouldn't have gone out of your way. I could have picked it up." She knew how busy he was. Everyone in the township knew that.

"No problem." He drew his coat a little more tightly around him, as if feeling the cold. "I've been meaning to see how you're getting along. This is an ambitious project you and your grandmother have launched."

"Yes, it is." He didn't know how ambitious. "But Grams is enjoying it."

"That's good." His eyes seemed distracted behind the wire-rimmed glasses he wore, his face lined and tired.

He wore himself out for everyone else. People said he'd turned down prestigious offers to come back to Churchville and become a family doctor, because the village and the surrounding area needed him.

"I understand you have old Mr. Hostetler's grandson staying here." He rocked back and forth on his heels. "I suppose he's come to put the farm on the market."

"I don't know what his plans are. Probably he'll sell the land. The house is in such bad shape, I'm not sure anyone would want it."

"He should just tear it down. Every old house isn't worth saving, like this one. You're doing a fine job with it."

"Thank you." She resisted the urge to confide how uncertain she was about her course. She wasn't his patient, and her problems weren't medical. She waved the envelope—no doubt Sandra's notes on the town brochure. "Please tell your wife I'll get right on this."

"I'll do that." He turned, heading for his car quickly, as if eager to turn on the heater.

Even as he got into his sedan, she saw Tyler's car pulling into the driveway. If he'd arrived a few minutes earlier, she could have introduced them.

"Was that a new guest?" Tyler came toward her across the crisp grass.

"Unfortunately not. That was Dr. Whitmoyer. You met his wife last night."

"So that's the good doctor."

"He really is. Good, I mean. He's the only doctor in the village, and in addition to carrying a huge patient load, he's doing valuable research on genetic diseases among the Amish."

"I'll agree that he's a paragon if you'll come inside for a few minutes." He was frowning. "I need to talk to you."

Now that she focused on him, she could sense his tension. Something was wrong.

She put down the ribbon she'd been holding. "Of course."

The warm air that greeted her when she walked inside made her fingers tingle. She led the way to the library, shrugging out of her jacket, and turned to face him. "What is it? Can I help you with something?"

He shoved his hands into his pockets, frowning, and ignored the invitation to sit. "I saw the attorney who's been handling things since my grandfather died. According to him, your grandfather tried to buy the farm at least six times since then."

She didn't understand the tone of accusation in his voice. "I suppose that's true. The neighbors weren't happy to see the place falling to pieces. It would be natural for my grandfather to make an offer for it."

"It sounds to me as if he was eager to snap up the property once my grandfather was out of the way. According to my mother, he and my grandfather had been feuding for years."

She planted her hands on her hips. There weren't many things that made her fighting mad, but innuendos about her family certainly did. "I'm not sure what you're driving at, Tyler. I don't know anything about any feud, but if it did exist, it's been over for twenty years or so. What does that matter now?"

His eyes seemed to darken. "It mattered to my mother. She talked to me about it before she died. She said her father told her someone was trying to cheat him out of what was his. That she didn't believe his death was as a result of a simple robbery. And that she believed the Unger family was involved."

THREE

Rachel's reaction to his statement was obvious. Shock battled anger for control.

That was what he'd felt, too, since the attorney told him about old Mr. Unger's attempt to buy the place. He'd hoped the lawyer would say his mother had been imagining things. Instead, his words seemed to confirm her suspicions.

Rachel took a breath, obviously trying to control her anger. She held both hands out, palms pushing away, her expression that of one who tries to calm a maniac. "I think you should leave now."

"And give you time to come up with a reasonable explanation? I'd rather have the truth."

Her green eyes sparked fire. "I don't need to come up with anything. You're the one making ridiculous accusations."

"Is it ridiculous? My grandfather claimed someone was trying to cheat him. Your grandfather tried repeatedly to buy his property. How else do you add those things up?"

"Not the way you do, obviously. There's a difference between buying and cheating someone. If your grandfather thought the offer low, he didn't have to sell." She flung out a hand toward the portrait that hung over the fireplace mantel. "Look at my grandfather. Does he look like someone who'd try to cheat a neighbor?"

"Appearances can be deceiving." Still, he had to admit that the face staring out from the frame had a quality of judicious fairness that made the idea seem remote.

She gave a quick shake of her head, as if giving up on him. "This is getting us nowhere. I'm sorry for your problems, but I can't help you. I'll be glad to refund your money if you want to check out." She stood very stiffly, her face pale and set.

He'd blown it. He'd acted on impulse, blurting out his suspicions, and now he wouldn't get a thing from her. Time to regroup.

"Look, I'm sorry for coming out with it that way. Can we sit down and talk this over rationally?"

Anger flashed in those green eyes. "Now you want to be rational? You're the one who started this with your ridiculous accusations."

He took a breath. He needed cooperation from Rachel if he were going to get anywhere. "Believe it or not, I felt as if I'd been hit by a two-by-four when I heard what Grassley, the attorney, had to say. Just hear me out. Then I'll leave if you want."

Rachel looked as if she were counting to ten. Finally she nodded. She waved him to the sofa and pulled the desk chair over for herself. She sat, planting her hands on its arms and looking ready to launch herself out of the chair at the slightest wrong word.

He sat on the edge of the sofa, trying to pull his thoughts into some sort of order. He was a logical person, so why couldn't he approach this situation logically?

Maybe he knew the answer to that one. Grief and guilt could be a powerful combination. He'd never realized how strong until the past few weeks.

"You have to understand—I had no idea all this was festering in my mother's mind. She didn't talk about her childhood, and I barely knew her father. I'd been here once, before I came for my grandfather's funeral."

She nodded. "You told me that. I thought then that there must have been some breach between your mother and your grandfather."

So she'd seen immediately what he'd have recognized if he weren't so used to the situation. "I never knew anything about it. My father may have known, but he died when I was in high school."

"I'm sorry." Her eyes darkened with sympathy, in spite of the fact that she must still be angry with him.

"My mother had always been—" He struggled to find the right word. "Secretive, I guess you'd say. After my father died, she started turning to me more. Change the lightbulbs, have the car serviced, talk to the neighbors about their barking dog. But she never shared anything about her finances or business matters. I knew my father had left her well off, so I didn't pry. That's why I didn't have any idea she still owned the property here."

"I suppose she let the attorney take care of

anything that had to be done. I'm surprised he didn't urge her to sell—to my grandfather or anyone else." Her voice was tart.

"He did, apparently, but he said she'd never even discuss it. She didn't with me until her illness." It had been hard to see her go downhill so quickly, hard to believe that none of the treatments were doing any good.

"What was it?"

"Cancer. When she realized she wasn't recovering, that's when she started to talk." He paused. "She'd left it late. She was on pain medication, not making much sense. But she said what I told you—that her father had insisted he was being cheated, that everyone was out to take advantage of him."

"That sounds as if he felt—well, that he thought he was being persecuted. How can you know that any of what he told her was true?"

"I can't. But she thought there were things about his death that had never been explained. She regretted that she'd never attempted to find out. She demanded my promise that I'd try to learn the truth."

His hands clenched. He'd told Rachel more than he'd intended. If she knew about what had happened then—but that was ridiculous. She'd been a child twenty-two years ago. At most, she'd oppose him now out of a need to protect her grandfather's reputation.

"I can understand why you feel you have to honor her wishes," she said, looking as if she chose her words carefully. "But after all this time, how can you possibly hope to learn anything?"

"I thought I might talk to your grandmother—"

"No!" She flared up instantly at that. "I won't have my grandmother upset by this."

A step sounded from the hallway, and they both turned. "That is not your decision to make, Rachel." Rachel's grandmother stood in the doorway, her bearing regal, her face set and stern.

Rachel's throat tightened. Grams, standing there, hearing the suspicions Tyler was voicing. She'd like to throw something at him for causing all this trouble, but that wouldn't help.

"Now, Grams…" She had to think of something that would repair this situation. Protecting Grams was her responsibility.

She stood and went to her, the desk chair rolling backward from the pressure of her hands. She put her arm around her grandmother's waist.

Grams didn't seem to need her support. She had pride and dignity to keep her upright.

"Don't 'now, Grams,' me, Rachel Elizabeth. I know what I heard, and I don't require any soothing platitudes."

Rachel shot a fulminating glance at Tyler. At least he had the grace to look unhappy at this turn of events. He'd look worse when she finished telling him what she thought.

"Grams, I'm sure you misunderstood." She tried for a light tone. "You always told us that eavesdroppers never hear anything good, remember?"

Grams ignored her, staring steadily at Tyler. "I must apologize. I'm not in the habit of listening in on other people's conversations, but you were both too busy arguing to realize I was there."

"I just want to protect you—" Rachel began.

Her grandmother cut her short with a look. "I don't require protection. I knew my husband well enough to be quite confident that he'd never have been involved in anything underhanded. I have nothing to fear from Mr. Dunn's inquiry."

"Of course not, but it's still upsetting. Please, Grams, let me handle this."

Her only response was to move to her armchair and be seated, folding her hands in her lap. "I'll answer any question you wish to ask." She glanced up at the portrait. "The truth can't harm my husband."

Grams might want to believe that, but Rachel wasn't so sure. Of course she knew Grandfather had been perfectly honest, but rumors, once started, could be difficult to stop.

She glanced at Tyler. He looked as if getting what he wanted had taken him by surprise.

"It's very good of you to agree to talk with me about this." He'd apparently decided on a formal approach. Good. If she caught the slightest whiff of disrespect, he'd be out of here before he knew what hit him.

Grams inclined her head graciously. "I don't know that I have much to offer. My husband only discussed business with me in very general terms."

Tyler's mouth tightened fractionally. "Start by telling me what you remember about John Hostetler. You must have known him, since you were such close neighbors."

"I knew him. Knew of him, certainly. He was a rather difficult person, from everything I recall. After his wife died, he became bitter, cutting himself off from the community."

"Do you know if your husband had any business dealings with him? Did he talk to you about wanting to buy the place?"

She frowned. "I don't remember, but if he did, it would be in his ledgers. Rachel will make them available to you."

She swallowed the protest that sprang to her lips. Tyler could strain his eyes looking through decades of her grandfather's fine black script, and he wouldn't find anything wrong.

"That's kind of you." Tyler seemed taken aback by that kindness, but that was her grandmother. "Do you know of anyone he was on bad terms with?"

A faint smile rippled on Grams's expression. "It might be easier to ask with whom he didn't quarrel. I don't mean to speak ill of him, but it's fairly well known that he argued with just about everyone."

"I remember a visit we made when I was about six. Certainly he and my mother seemed to battle most of the time."

"I'm afraid that was his nature." Grams spread her hands. "I don't know what else I can say. After his death, the neighbors were concerned about the condition of the farm. Several of them came to Fredrick about it, I remember that." She glanced up at the portrait again. "If he did try to buy it, I'm sure that's why."

He nodded, not offering any comment. It was what

Rachel had told him, too, but she didn't think he was convinced. He wouldn't understand her grandfather's almost-feudal-lord position in the community. Everyone, Amish and English alike, had come to him with their concerns.

"Do you remember anything about the robbery and his death?"

Grams moved slightly, and Rachel was instantly on the alert. This questioning bothered her grandmother more than she'd want to admit.

"I know we were shocked. Everyone was."

She put her arm around her grandmother. "Of course they were." She darted him a look. "I think my grandmother has told you everything she can."

Grams gave Tyler a level look. "I have, but if there's anything else…"

"Not right now." Tyler seemed to know he'd pushed enough.

Grams rose. "We'll cooperate in any way we can. It's what my husband would wish." She turned toward the kitchen and walked away steadily.

Rachel hesitated. She wanted his promise that this wasn't going to be all over the township by sunset, but she didn't want to say that where Grams could hear. She'd better make sure Grams was safely in the kitchen with Emma.

"Would you mind sticking around for a minute or two while I speak to Emma? I could use some help moving that ladder."

He nodded, his expression telling her he understood what she wasn't saying. "I'll wait for you outside."

* * *

By the time she went out the front door a few minutes later, Rachel knew exactly how she should behave. She'd talk with Tyler very calmly, explaining the harm that could be done to her grandmother by careless talk. She'd make it clear that they'd already done everything he'd asked of them and that there really was nothing else they could contribute.

She would not express the anger she felt. She'd extended friendship to the man, and all the time he'd been using her to pry into her family.

He waited by the ladder she'd left propped against the house, his leather jacket hanging open in the warmth of the afternoon sunshine. He straightened when he saw her. "Is your grandmother all right?"

"She didn't like being cross-examined," she said sharply, and then snapped her mouth shut on the words. If she wanted discretion from Tyler, she'd better try a little tact of her own. "She was telling you the truth." Katherine Unger was not someone who'd lie to cover up her own or anyone else's misdeeds.

He gave her a slight smile. "I know. Do you think I don't recognize integrity when I see it?"

"I was afraid your judgment might be skewed by your need to find out about your grandfather."

"Look, I said I was sorry for jumping on you with it. I want to be fair about it."

Did he mean that? She hoped so. "There's one thing you said to me that you didn't mention to my grandmother."

He frowned. "What's that?"

He knew. He had to. "You said your mother didn't think her father's death had been adequately explained. You called it murder."

The word seemed to stand there between them, stark and ugly.

He was silent for a long moment, and then he shook his head. "I don't know, Rachel. That's the truth. I can tell you what my mother said. What she seemed to believe. As to whether it had any basis in fact—" he shrugged "—I guess that's what I have to find out."

"I hope—" She stopped. Would he think she was trying to control his actions? Well, in a way, she was.

"What do you hope?" He focused on her, eyes intent.

"I hope you'll be discreet with the questions you ask people around here, especially anything to do with my grandparents. It doesn't take much to set rumors flying in a small community like this."

"Your grandmother didn't seem to be worried about that."

No, she wouldn't worry about people talking when she felt she was doing what was right.

"Grams can be naive about some things. If the rumor mill starts churning, the situation will be difficult for her. So be tactful, will you please?"

"I'll try." He took a step back from the wooden stepladder as she approached it. "I'm not here to stir up trouble for innocent people."

"Sometimes innocent people get hurt by the backlash." She bent to plug the end of the string of lights into the outlet.

"I can't let that stop me from looking for the truth." His jaw set like a stone.

"And I won't let anything stop me from protecting my family," she said. "Just so we're clear."

"We're clear. Does that mean you want me to move out?"

It was tempting to say yes, but it was safer to have Tyler where she could keep track of him. "You're welcome to stay as long as you want." She started up the ladder, the loop of lights in her hand.

"Thank you. And since I'm staying, I'd be glad to climb up and do that for you. I wouldn't have to stretch as far."

"I can reach." If she stood on the top step on her tiptoes, she could.

She looped the string of lights over the small metal hook that was left in the window frame from year to year. Pulling the string taut, she grasped it and leaned toward the other side.

She stretched, aware of him watching her, and pushed the wire toward the hook—

"Wait!" Tyler barked.

The wire touched the hook—a sharp snap, a scent of burning, a jolt that knocked her backward off the ladder and sent her flying toward the ground, stunned.

FOUR

"**I**'m fine. Really." Rachel tried to muster a convincing tone, but if she looked half as shaken as she felt, it was hardly surprising that Tyler wanted to rush her to the hospital.

"You don't look fine." He had a firm hold on her arm, and he didn't seem inclined to let go any time soon. "My car's right there. If you won't go to the E.R., at least let that local doctor you were talking to have a look."

"I don't need Dr. Whitmoyer to look at me." She rubbed her hands together, trying to get rid of the tingling sensation. "It just knocked the wind out of me, that's all."

He still seemed doubtful, but finally he gave a reluctant nod. "I'll help you inside."

"No." She tried to pull her arm free, but he continued to propel her toward the door. "Look, I don't want my grandmother upset, okay? She's been worried enough about me since the accident, and the last thing she needs is any fresh reason to fear. Besides, she's already had her quota of crises today."

Tyler's face settled in a frown, but at least he stopped pulling her toward the door. "That's dirty pool, you know that?"

"I'll do whatever works where Grams is concerned. She may think she's still as tough as she always was, but that's not true."

After her accident and then Andrea's brush with death in the early summer, Grams had shown a fragility that had hit both of them hard. She was doing much better now—confident that the inn would succeed, happy about Andrea's wedding. Nothing must disrupt that.

Tyler urged her toward the step. "Sit down and get your breath back, at least. When I saw the power arc and you fly backward, I thought my heart would stop."

"Sorry about that." She managed a smile as she sank down on the low stone step. It was nice of him to be so concerned about her. "I felt a bit scared myself, not that I had time to think about it. Is it my imagination, or did you tell me to stop just before I touched the hook?"

He nodded, putting one foot on the step and leaning his elbow on his knee as he bent toward her. "A second too late. I caught a glimpse of bare wire where the sun glinted on it. Sorry I didn't see it sooner. And sorry you didn't think to check those lights before you plugged them in."

"I'll admit that wasn't the smartest thing I ever did, but I did look over them when I got the box out of the attic. At least—" She stopped, thinking about it.

"Well?"

She glared at him. "I think I checked them, but I was

in a rush to get ready for last night's meeting." She'd shoved the box in the downstairs restroom when she'd realized how late it was. Maybe she had missed some of the strings.

Tyler, apparently feeling it wiser not to pursue the conversation, walked over to the stepladder and cautiously detached the string of lights. He frowned down at it for a moment before carrying it back to her.

"There's the culprit." He held the strand between his hands. Green plastic coating had melted away from a foot-long stretch of cord, and the wire between was blackened and mangled, shreds of metal twisting up like frizzled hair. The acrid smell of it turned her stomach.

"Guess I won't be using that string of lights anytime soon." It took an effort to speak lightly.

"Or ever." He was still frowning, the cord stretched taut between his hands. "That's a lot of bare wire."

She shrugged, trying to push away the creeping sensation on the back of her neck. "All's well that ends well. I'm relatively unscathed, and I'd better get back to work."

"Sit still." He softened the command with a half smile. "Sorry, but you look washed out."

"Gee, thanks."

Now he grinned, his face relaxing. "Just let me see if this blew a fuse before you do anything else."

She hadn't even thought of that, so she leaned back against the step, watching him test the heavy-duty extension cord on a fresh strip of lights.

"Looks okay. Actually that's surprising. Usually the wiring in these old places isn't in great shape."

"You should see the maze of wires in the cellar. It's

an electrician's nightmare, but it all seems to work. We did have to have the wiring checked out before we could open the inn, of course."

He gazed up at the house. "It's early eighteenth century, isn't it?"

"I guess an architect would know. The oldest part dates to 1725, according to the records."

"It's been in your family ever since?"

"Pretty much. My maternal grandfather's family, the Ungers, that is."

He was probably making conversation to distract her from the fact that he was going over each strand of lights in the box, checking all of them methodically with eyes and hands.

Well, she wouldn't object to that. She was happy enough just to sit here, feeling the sun's warmth chase the winter chill away.

"Satisfied?" she asked when he'd put gone through every one.

"They're in better shape than I expected." He frowned a little. "You'd think if one was that bad, some of the others would show similar signs."

"Maybe a squirrel tried to make a meal of it, didn't like the taste, and left the rest alone."

"Could be." He picked up a strand of lights and mounted the stepladder.

"What are you doing?" She stood, fighting a wave of dizziness at the sudden movement. "I'll take care of that."

"I've got it."

She'd keep arguing, but he really was getting the

job accomplished more easily than she could, given his height. She watched, liking the neat efficiency of his movements, the capability of his strong hands. She was used to doing for herself, and in the months of running the inn she'd learned how to do all kinds of things she'd never dreamed of before, but it was nice to have some help.

She couldn't rely on him. Not Tyler, of all people, given what brought him here. That galvanized her, and she went quickly to the stepladder.

"I'm sure you have work of your own to do." Such as investigating his grandfather's death.

"This is the least I can do, since your grandmother offered your cooperation in dealing with my problem."

"That's not exactly what she said."

He smiled faintly but continued to thread the cord through the hooks.

And if she did help him, what then? She was as convinced as Grams that Grandfather hadn't done anything wrong.

She watched Tyler, frowning a little, trying to pinpoint the cause of her uneasiness. No matter how irrational it was, she couldn't help feeling that Tyler's determination to look into his grandfather's death was similar to poking a stick into a hornet's nest.

Rachel searched through the changes she was attempting to make to the inn's Web site. Did she have everything right? Andrea could probably have done this in half an hour, but she'd been working for what seemed like hours.

She glanced at the ornate German mantel clock that stood on one side of her grandfather's portrait above the fireplace. Nearly ten. It *had* been hours. Grams had gone up to bed some time ago, but Barney still dozed on the hearth rug, keeping her company.

She smiled at the sheltie, and he lifted his head and looked at her as if he'd sensed her movement. "Just a little longer, Barney. I'm almost finished."

He put his head back on his front paws, as if he'd understood every word.

Tyler had gone out earlier and hadn't come back yet. She certainly wouldn't wait up for him, although she'd had difficulty all summer going to bed when guests were still out. He had a key—he'd let himself in.

Thinking about that opened the door to thoughts of him, just when she'd succeeded in submerging her concerns about Tyler in her more prosaic worries.

If she could stay angry with him, dealing with the situation might be easier. Unfortunately, each time he had her thoroughly riled, he managed to show her some side of himself that roused her sympathy.

Tyler was determined to give this quest his best effort, and she'd guess he brought that same single-minded attention to every project he undertook. That would be an asset in his profession, but at the moment she wished he were more easily distracted.

He'd had a difficult relationship with his mother— that much was clear. She sympathized, given her own mother, who was as careless with people as she was with things. She'd always had the sense that her mother could have left her behind on one of their frequent moves and not even noticed she was gone. Not that Andrea would have let that happen.

She rubbed her temples, trying to ease away the tightness there.

I'm spinning in circles, Lord, and I don't know how to stop. Please help me see Tyler through Your eyes and understand how to deal with him in the way You want.

Even as she finished the prayer, she heard the sound of the door opening and closing, followed by Tyler's step in the hallway. She paused, fingers on the keyboard, listening for him to go up the stairs.

Instead he swung the library door a bit farther open and looked around it. "Still working? I didn't realize bed-and-breakfast proprietors kept such late hours."

"It's pretty much a twenty-four-hour-a-day job, but at the moment I'm just trying to finish up some changes to the Web page. Not my strong suit, I'm afraid."

"Mind if I have a look?" He hesitated, seeming to wait for an invitation.

"Please. I think I have it right, but I'm almost afraid to try and upload it."

He smiled, putting one hand on the back of her chair and leaning over to stare at the screen.

"Never let the computer know you're afraid of it. That's when it will do something totally unexpected."

"Just about anything to do with it is unexpected as far as I'm concerned. I'd still be keeping reservations in a handwritten log if Andrea hadn't intervened."

"Andrea. That's the older sister, right?" He reached around her to touch the keyboard, correcting a typo she hadn't noticed.

"Two years older." She tried not to think about how close he was. "She and her new husband are on their honeymoon. Somehow I don't think I can call and ask her computer questions at the moment."

"Probably wouldn't be diplomatic," he agreed. "As far as I can see, this looks ready. All you have to do is upload."

She hesitated, cursor poised. "That's it?"

"Just click." He smiled down at her, giving her a slightly inverted view of his face, exposing a tiny scar on his square chin that she hadn't noticed before.

And shouldn't be noticing now. She was entirely too aware of him for her own peace of mind.

She forced her attention back to the computer and pressed the button, starting the upload. "I can see you're a fixer, just like my big sister. She's always willing to take over and do something for the inept."

As soon as the words were out of her mouth, she heard how they sounded and was embarrassed. She thought she'd gotten over the feeling that she would never measure up to Andrea. And if she hadn't, she certainly didn't want to sound insecure to Tyler.

"There's nothing wrong with admitting you don't know how to do something. I couldn't make a quiche if someone offered me a million bucks."

"It's nice of you to put it that way." She leaned back, looking with faint surprise at the updated Web site. "It actually worked."

"You sound impressed. The program you're using is pretty much 'what you see is what you get.'"

"I seem to remember Andrea saying that. She

actually told me how to do it, but my brain doesn't retain things like that."

Tyler's smile flickered. "Maybe you should write it up as if it's a recipe."

"Just might work." She smiled up at him, relaxing now that the work was done. For a moment time seemed to halt. She was lost in the deep blue of his eyes, the room so quiet she could hear his breathing.

She drew in a strangled breath of her own and broke the eye contact, grateful he couldn't know how her pulse was pounding.

That was unexpected. Or was it? Hadn't the attraction been there, underlying the tension, each time they were together?

Tyler cleared his throat. "You know, you could hire someone to run the Web site for you." He seemed to be talking at random, as much at a loss as she was.

Oddly enough, that helped her regain her poise. "Can't afford it," she said bluntly. "We're operating on a shoestring as it is, and it's getting a bit frayed at the moment."

He blinked. "I didn't realize. I mean—" His gesture took in the room, but she understood that he meant the house and grounds, too. "People who live in places like this often don't have to count their pennies."

"That's why it's a bed-and-breakfast." She wasn't usually so forthcoming, but it wasn't anything that everyone in the township didn't already know. And probably would be happy to gossip about. "If Grams is going to keep the place, this seems her only option.

Luckily, she's a born hostess, and she's enjoying it. Otherwise, she'd have to sell."

"She doesn't want to do that, so you feel you have to help her."

"Not exactly. I mean, I love it, too." Was it possible he'd understand her feelings? "But even if I didn't, Grams was always there for us when our parents weren't. I owe her."

"I take it your folks had a rocky marriage."

"You could say that. My father left more times than I can count, until finally he just didn't come back."

"That's when you lived with your grandparents?"

She nodded. "They were our rock. Now it's our turn. I'll do whatever is necessary to make this work for Grams."

His face seemed to become guarded, although his voice, when he spoke, was light. "Even if it means learning how to do the Web site."

"Only until Andrea comes back." She frowned, thinking of yet another chore. "I guess I really should put some Christmas photos up, too. She and Cal won't be home in time to do that."

"If you get stuck, just give me a shout." He turned away, his expression still somehow distant.

Some barrier had gone up between them, and she wasn't sure why. Because of her determination to take care of her grandmother, and he equated that with interference in what he planned? If so, he was right.

He paused at the door, glancing back at her. "Good night, Rachel. Don't work too hard."

"Thanks again for the help."

He vanished behind the partially open door, and she heard his steady footsteps mounting the stairs.

If she let herself start thinking about Tyler's situation, she'd never sleep tonight. "Come on, Barney." She clicked her fingers at the dog. "Let's go to bed. We'll worry about it tomorrow."

It was unusual to be unable to concentrate on work. Tyler had always prided himself on his ability to shut out everything in order to focus on the job at hand, but not this time.

He closed the computer file and shut down his laptop. No, not this time. Before he came to Churchville, he'd thought the task he'd set himself, although probably impossible, was at least fairly straightforward. Find out what he could about his grandfather's death, deal with the property, go back to his normal life with his conscience intact.

He hadn't counted on the human element. Everyone he'd met since he arrived seemed to have a stake in his actions—or at least an opinion as to his choices.

Restless, he moved to the window that overlooked the street, folding back the shutters, and leaned on the deep windowsill. The innkeeper, the antique dealer, the doctor's wife—it sounded like a ridiculous version of doctor, lawyer, Indian chief.

He glanced down the road in the direction of the antique shop, but there was nothing to be seen. Churchville slept. Not even a car went by to disturb the night. He'd heard of places so small they rolled up the sidewalks at night. Churchville was apparently one of them.

Presumably Rachel and her grandmother were asleep as well, off in the other wing of the building.

He couldn't help wondering how she'd adjusted from the pressure-cooker atmosphere of a trendy restaurant kitchen to the grueling work but slower pace of running a B&B in the Pennsylvania Dutch countryside. Still, she'd shown him how dedicated she was.

Dedicated to her family, most of all. And yet, from what she'd said, her relationship with her father had been as strained as his with his mother. Maybe that made her other relatives more precious to her.

At least he'd eventually grown up enough to pity his mother for resorting to emotional blackmail with the people she loved. He'd learned to look at her demands in a more objective way. But now he was back in the same trap, trying to fulfill her impossible dying request. No, not request. Demand.

Looked at rationally, the proposal was ridiculous. He'd known that from the start, even colored as the moment had been by shock and grief.

Still, he'd had to deal with the property, and he'd told himself he'd find out what he could about the circumstances of his grandfather's death and then close the book on the whole sad story.

Now that he was here, he realized how much more difficult the situation was than he'd dreamed. Rachel's grandmother's integrity was obvious, and he couldn't imagine her covering up a crime, any more than he could imagine the personality that dominated the portrait over the mantel committing one.

This was a wild-goose chase. A sad one, but nothing

more. Moreover, it could hurt innocent people, if Rachel's opinion was true, and he saw no reason to doubt that.

He closed the shutters again, feeling as if he were closing his mind to the whole uncomfortable business. He'd make a few inquiries, maybe talk to the local police and check the newspaper files. And at the end of it he'd be no wiser than he was now.

The shutters still stood open on the window that looked out the side of the house, so he went to close them. And stopped, hand arrested on the louvered wood.

Where was that light coming from?

Below him was the gravel sweep of the drive, well-lit by the security lighting, his car a dark bulk. There was the garage, beyond it the lane that led onto Crossings Road.

The pale ribbon of road dipped down into the trees. From ground level, he wouldn't have seen any farther, but from this height the shallow bowl of the valley stretched out. As his eyes grew accustomed to the dimness, he could make out the paler patches of fields, darker shadows of woods. That had to be the farmhouse—there was nothing else down on that stretch of road.

A faint light flickered, was gone, reappeared again. Not at ground level. Someone was in the house, moving around the second floor with a flashlight.

He spun, grabbing his car keys, and rushed into the hall. He pounded down the stairs, relieved there were no other guests to be disturbed by him.

In the downstairs hall he paused briefly. He should

call the police before heading out, should tell Rachel what was going on before she heard him and thought someone was breaking in.

He tried the library door, found it unlocked, and hurried through to the separate staircase that must lead to the family bedrooms. If she was still awake—

A light shone down from an upstairs hall.

"Rachel?"

Soft footsteps, and she appeared at the top of the stairs, clutching a cell phone in one hand. At least she was still dressed, so he hadn't gotten her out of bed.

"What's wrong?" Her eyes were wide with apprehension.

"Someone's in my grandfather's house. I could see the light from my window."

She didn't try to argue about it, but hurried down the steps, dialing the phone as she did. "I'll call the police."

"Good. I'm going down there."

She grabbed his arm. "Wait. You don't know what you might be rushing into."

"That's what I'm going to find out." He shook off her hand. "Just tell the cops I'm there, so they don't think I'm the burglar."

He strode toward the back door, hearing her speaking, presumably to the 911 operator, as he let the door close behind him.

He jogged toward the car, a chill wind speeding his steps. This could be nothing more than some teenage vandals.

And if it was someone else?

Well then, he'd know he'd been wrong. He'd know there was something to investigate after all.

He took off down the lane, gravel spurting under his tires. A clump of bushes came rushing at him as the lane turned, and he forced himself to ease off the gas. Wouldn't do any good for him to smash into a tree.

Rachel's accident slid into his mind, displacing his concentration on the prowler. An image of her, standing in the road, whirling, face white, to stare in horror at the oncoming car—

He shook his head, taking a firm control on both thoughts and reactions. Get to the farm in one piece. Find out what was happening. Hope the cops got there in time to back him up.

The car rounded the final bend, and the dilapidated gateposts came into view. He stepped on the brake, took the turn cautiously and then snapped off his headlights. He couldn't have done it earlier, not without smashing up, but he could probably get up the lane without lights. He didn't want to alert the prowlers to his presence too soon. They could hear the motor, of course, but they might attribute that to a car going past on the lane. Headlights glaring at them would be a dead giveaway.

If they were still there. He frowned, squinting in the dim light of a waning moon. He could make out the rectangular bulk of the house, gray in the faint light, and the darker bulk behind it that was the barn. No sign of a vehicle—no glimmer of metal to give it away. It looked as if he was too late.

He drew to a stop next to the porch, cut the motor,

opened the door and listened. No sound broke the night silence, not even a bird. He got out, moving cautiously, alert for any sign of the intruder.

Still nothing. He walked toward the steps. Stupid, to have come without a decent torch. He had only the small penlight on his keychain to show him the broken stair. He stepped over it, mounting the porch, the wooden planks creaking beneath his feet.

He focused the thin stream of light on the door, senses alert. It seemed to be as securely closed as it had been on his first visit. A flick of the light showed him boards secure over the windows.

The urgency that had driven him this far ebbed, leaving him feeling cold and maybe a little foolish. Could the light he'd seen have been some sort of reflection? He wouldn't think so.

Well, assuming someone had been here, they were gone now. Maybe he could at least figure out how they'd gotten in.

He bent, aiming the feeble light at the lock. Had those scratches—

A board creaked behind him. Muscles tightening, he started to swing around. A shadowy glimpse of a dark figure, an upraised arm, and then something crashed into his head and the floor came up to meet him.

FIVE

Given the small size of the township police force, Rachel knew her call would go straight through to whoever was on duty. Thankfulness swept her at the sound of Chief Burkhalter's competent voice.

It took only seconds to explain, but even so she was aware of how quickly Tyler would reach the farm. And put himself in danger.

"My guest, Tyler Dunn, the one who saw the lights—"

"Owns the farm. Right, I know."

Of course he would. Zachary Burkhalter made it his business to know what went on in the township.

"He's gone down there. Don't—"

"I'm not going to shoot him, Ms. Hampton, but he's an idiot. I'll be there in a few minutes."

And she could hear the wail of the siren now, through the air as well as the telephone. She could also hear Grams coming out of her bedroom.

"I could go down—" Rachel began, with some incoherent thought of identifying Tyler to the chief.

"No." The snapped word left no doubt in her mind. "I'll call you back on this line when we've cleared the place. Then you can come pick up your straying guest, but not until then."

She had no choice but to disconnect. The change in tone of the siren's wail as it turned down Crossings Road was reassuring. They'd be there soon. Tyler would be all right.

Grams reached her. "What is it, Rachel? What's happening?"

Rachel put her arm around Grams, as much for her comfort as her grandmother's. "Tyler saw a light moving around in the farmhouse. He insisted on going down there by himself, but the police are on their way."

Grams shook her head. "Foolish, but I suppose he wouldn't be one to sit back when there's trouble."

No, he probably wouldn't. It didn't take a long acquaintance with Tyler to know that much about him.

"I still wish he hadn't. If he runs right into who-ever's there—"

"I'm sure he'll be sensible about it." Grams's voice was matter-of-fact. "The police are probably there by now."

She'd thought she'd have to comfort her grand-mother, but it seemed to be working the other way around. Grams patted her shoulder.

"I'll start some hot chocolate. He'll be chilled to the bone, I shouldn't wonder, running out on a cold night like this."

She followed Grams to the kitchen, phone still in

her hand, watching as her grandmother paused for a moment, head bowed.

Dear Lord, I should be turning to You, too, instead of letting worry eat at me. Please, be with Tyler and protect him from harm.

Even as she finished the prayer, the telephone rang. Exchanging glances with Grams, she answered.

"You can come on down here now, if you want." The chief sounded exasperated, which probably meant they hadn't been in time to catch anyone. "Maybe help Mr. Dunn figure out what's missing."

Questions hovered on her tongue, but better to wait until she saw what was going on. "I'll be right there."

It took a moment to reassure Grams that she'd be perfectly safe, another to grab her jacket and shove Barney back from the door, and she ran out and slid into the car, shivering a little.

She shot out the drive and turned onto Crossings Road with only a slight qualm as she passed the place where she'd been hit.

Why? The question beat in her brain as she drove down the road as quickly as the rough surface would allow. If someone was in the house, why? More specifically, why now? It had stood empty all these years and been broken into more than once. Why would someone break in now, when surely most people knew that the new owner was here?

Lots of questions. No answers.

She turned into the rutted lane that led to the farmhouse, slowing of necessity. The police car, its roof light still rotating, sat next to Tyler's car. Its headlights showed her Chief Burkhalter's tall figure, standing next to the porch.

Tyler sat on the edge of the porch, head bent, one hand massaging the back of his neck.

She pulled to a stop and slid out, hurrying toward them. "Are you all right?"

"I'm fine." Tyler frowned at the chief. "There was no need for him to call you."

"There was every need." She hoped her tone was brisk enough to disguise the wobble in her tummy. "You're hurt. Let me see."

Ignoring his protests, she ran her hand through the thick hair, feeling the lump gingerly.

He winced. "Are you a nurse as well as a chef?"

"No, but I know enough to be sure you should have some ice on that."

"I offered to take him to the E.R. or call paramedics," the chief said. "He turned me down."

"I don't need a doctor. I've had harder knocks than that on the football field. And the ice can wait until we've finished here."

"Just go over it once more for me," Burkhalter said, apparently accepting him at his word. "You saw the lights from your window at the inn, you said."

Tyler started to nod, then seemed to think better of it. "The side window of my room looks out over Crossings Road. I can see the house—or at least, the upper floor of it. I spotted what looked like a flashlight moving around on the second floor."

"So you decided to investigate for yourself." Burkhalter sounded resigned, as if he'd taken Tyler's measure already.

"I figured I could get here faster than you could."

She wanted to tell Tyler how foolish that had been, but his aching head was probably doing that well enough. Besides, she had no standing—they were nothing more than acquaintances. The reminder gave her a sense of surprise. She'd begun to feel as if she'd known him for years.

"What did you see when you got here?"

"No vehicle, so I thought maybe they'd gone already. My mistake." Tyler grimaced. "I went to look at the front door, to see if it had been broken into, and while I was bending over, somebody hit me from behind."

"You didn't get a look, I suppose."

"Only at the floorboards." Tyler massaged the back of his neck again. "I heard the car come round the house then. They must have parked it in the back. The guy who slugged me jumped in, and off they went. I managed to turn my head at some point, but all I could see were red taillights disappearing down the lane."

"Vehicle was parked by the kitchen door." The patrolman who joined them gave Rachel a shy smile. "Looks like a big SUV, maybe, by the size of the tires. They broke in the back."

"I should have gone around the house first." Tyler sounded annoyed with himself. "I didn't think."

"Wait for us next time," the chief said. "Not that I expect there to be a next time. If these were the same thieves who have broken into other empty houses, they won't be careless enough to come back again, now that they know someone's watching."

"This has happened before?" Tyler's gaze sharpened. "What are they after?"

"Anything they find of value. Old-timers in country places often don't think much of banks, so sometimes it's been strong boxes broken open. Other times silver or antiques."

Burkhalter's lean face tightened. At a guess, he didn't like the fact that someone had been getting away with burglaries in his territory. Nobody blamed him, surely. The township was far-flung, the police force spread too thin.

"If there's nothing else Mr. Dunn can tell you, maybe he ought to get in out of the cold." She was shivering a little, whether from the cold or the tension, and Tyler had rushed out in just a shirt and sweater.

"If you wouldn't mind taking a look around inside first, I'd appreciate it. See if anything's missing."

Tyler stood, holding on to the porch post for a moment. "Ms. Hampton and I were here yesterday, but we didn't go upstairs. And Philip Longstreet stopped while we were here, wanting to have a look around. I told him I'd let him know if I decided to sell anything."

Philip wouldn't be delighted to have his name brought up in the middle of a police investigation. Still, there was no reason for Tyler to hold the information back.

The chief's expression didn't betray whether that interested him or not. He ushered them inside and swung his light around, letting them see the contents of the living room.

In the daylight the place had looked bad enough. In the cold and dark it was desolate, but as far as she could tell, nothing had been moved.

"I think this is pretty much the way it was. Tyler?"

He seemed tenser inside the house than he had sitting on the porch. He gave a short nod. "I don't think they were in this room."

They walked through the dining room, then into the kitchen. Everything seemed untouched, other than the fact that the kitchen door had been broken in.

The chief's strong flashlight beam touched the stairway that opened into the kitchen. "Let's have a look upstairs."

"I haven't been up there yet," Tyler warned. "I can't say I know everything that should be there."

"Anything you remember could help." The chief was polite but determined.

Tyler nodded and started up the stairs. She couldn't assist in the least, since she'd never been in that part of the house, but she didn't like the idea of staying downstairs alone. She followed them, watching her footing on the creaking stairs.

The flight of steps led into a small, square hallway with bedrooms leading off it. Tyler stopped, gripping the railing. "There used to be a slant-top desk there, I remember."

"Not recently." The chief swung his flashlight over the thick layer of dust that lay, undisturbed, where Tyler indicated.

They peered into one bedroom after another. There was more furniture up here, sturdy country pieces, most of it, some probably of interest to collectors. Tyler really should have it properly valued.

The thieves had evidently started in the master bedroom, where the dresser drawers gaped open and empty. A small marble-topped stand had been pulled away from the faded wallpaper, and a basin and ewer set lay smashed on the floor.

Rachel bent, touching a piece gingerly. "Too bad they broke this. There's been quite a demand recently for sets of this vintage."

"Maybe they weren't educated thieves," Tyler said.

"Or they just don't know about china."

Tyler stepped carefully over the pieces. "Seems like a stupid place for them to hit. Obviously there's no money or small valuables left. My impression is that the rooms used to be fairly crowded with furniture, but that's hardly going to let you trace anything."

"I don't suppose there's such a thing as an inventory," the chief asked.

"My grandfather's attorney did give me a list, but I don't know how complete it is." Tyler's smile flickered. "And given how little I know about Pennsylvania Dutch furniture, I doubt I could even figure out what's being described on the list."

"I can probably help you with that. Furnishing the inn made me something of an instant expert on the subject." She was faintly surprised to hear the offer coming out of her mouth. Didn't she already have enough to keep her busy?

"Sounds like a good idea," Chief Burkhalter said. "Let me have a copy of the list, and mark anything you and Ms. Hampton think has gone missing. At least that gives us a start."

His light illumined Tyler's face briefly. Was Tyler really that pale and strained, or was it just the effect of the glaring white light?

"You folks might as well get home." Burkhalter swung his torch to show them the way out. "We'll be a bit longer. Ms. Hampton, if you wouldn't mind taking Mr. Dunn, I'll have my officer drop his car off later. I don't think he should be driving."

"That's fine," she said, grabbing Tyler's arm before he could protest. "Let's go."

He must have been feeling fairly rocky, since he let her tug him down the stairs. When they reached the front porch, she took a deep breath of cold air. Even its bite was preferable to the stale, musty scent of decay inside.

No wonder Tyler disliked the place. His grandfather had been an unhappy, miserable man, by all accounts, and that unhappiness seemed to permeate the very walls of the house.

They stepped off the porch, and Tyler shivered a little when the wind hit him. He shoved his hands into his pockets. "So that's it. Minor-league housebreakers." He sounded— She wasn't sure what. Dissatisfied, maybe?

"I suppose so." She led the way to the car.

Maybe Tyler was thinking the same thing she was. Thieves, yes. That seemed logical.

But why now? That was the thing that bothered her the most. Why now?

* * *

"Are you sure you want to do this?" Tyler glanced at Rachel as they walked down Churchville's Main Street the next morning, headed for the antique shop.

She looked up at him, eyebrows lifting. "Why not? It'll be much easier for you to understand the look and value of the furniture on that list if you actually see some examples of Pennsylvania Dutch furniture. And the inn's furnishings aren't really the plain country pieces your grandfather had, for the most part. I have to pick up the final draft of the house tour brochure from Phillip, anyway."

"You're forgetting that I gave Phil Longstreet's name to the police last night. If they've come to call, he may not appreciate the sight of me."

"I'm sure Phil realizes that after the break-in, you had to mention anyone who'd been there. You certainly didn't accuse him of anything."

But he thought he read a certain reservation in her green eyes. She needed the goodwill of her fellow business people in the village. He'd been so focused on getting what he wanted that he hadn't considered how her efforts to help him might rebound against her.

"I don't want you to get involved in my troubles if it's going to make things sticky for you with people like Longstreet. And I sure don't want you involved if it means putting you at any risk."

They were on the opposite side of the road from the inn, because Rachel had wanted to take a digital photo of the inn's exterior decorations. He paused, turning to face her and leaning against the low stone wall that surrounded the church and cemetery.

"Because of what happened last night?" A frown puckered her smooth forehead. "But that was just—" She paused, shook her head. "I was going to say an accident, but it certainly wasn't that. Still, anyone who goes charging into a deserted house at night to investigate a prowler—"

"Deserves a lump on the head?" He touched the tender spot and smiled wryly. "You may have a point there. I just can't help but wonder if last night's episode had anything to do with my reason for being here."

She leaned against the wall next to him, her green corduroy jacket bright against the cream stone. Two cars went by before she spoke.

"Why now, that's what you mean. After all this time of sitting empty, why would someone choose to burglarize the place just when you've returned? I've been wondering about that myself."

She had a sharp mind behind that sensitive, heart-shaped face.

"Right. Assuming it had something to do with my return, or my reason for being here—"

She shook her head decisively. "Not that, surely. No one knows except Grams and me, and I assure you, neither of us goes in for late-night prowling. Everyone else thinks you're here just to sell the property."

He found he wanted to speak the thought that had been hovering at the back of his mind. "If someone had guilty knowledge of my grandfather's death, my coming to dispose of the property might still be alarming." He planted his hands against the top of the wall. "If there's even a chance of that, I shouldn't involve you."

"First of all, I think the chance that last night's thieves were in any way related to your grandfather's death twenty-some years ago is infinitesimal. And second, I'm not offering to mount guard on the farm at midnight. Helping you identify the furniture hardly seems like a threatening activity, does it?"

"Not when you put it that way. You're determined to help, aren't you?"

She nodded, but her mouth seemed to tighten. "Andrea is the superstar. Caro is the dreamer. I'm the one who helps."

"I didn't mean that negatively," he said mildly. "It's a quality I admire."

Her face relaxed in a genuine smile. "Then you're an unusual man." She pushed herself away from the wall. "Come on, let's put my helpfulness to use and check out some Pennsylvania Dutch antiques."

"Rachel?"

She glanced back at the query in his tone.

"Thanks. For the help."

"Anytime."

She started briskly down the street. He caught up with her in a few strides, and they walked in a companionable silence for a few minutes. Rachel was obviously taking note of the decorations on the shops, and twice she stopped to take photos.

"They've done a good job of making the place look

like an old-fashioned Christmas," he commented. "I like the streetlights."

Churchville's Main Street had gas streetlamps that reminded him of the illustration for a Dickens novel. Each one had been surrounded with a wreath of live greens and holly, tied with a burgundy ribbon.

"You're just lucky you weren't here for the arguments when we made that decision," she said. "I thought Sandra Whitmoyer and Phillip Longstreet would come to blows."

"I couldn't imagine people would get so excited about it."

She raised her eyebrows. "You mentioned that you sometimes design churches. Don't you get into some passionate debates on that subject?"

He thought of one committee that had nearly canceled the entire project because they couldn't agree on the shape of the education wing. "You have a point there. People do feel passionate about things that affect their church or their home. I suppose the same applies when you're talking about a village the size of Churchville. They all feel they have a stake in the outcome."

She nodded. "It surprised me a little, when I came back after spending a lot of time in an urban setting. At first it bothered me that everyone seemed to know everyone else's business, but then I realized it's not just about wanting to know. It's about caring."

He was unaccountably touched. "That's a nice tribute to your community."

"I like belonging."

The words were said quietly, but there was a depth

of feeling behind them that startled him. He would like to pursue it, but they'd come to a stop in front of Longstreet's Antiques, and Rachel's focus had obviously shifted to the job at hand.

"Don't show too much interest in any one thing," she warned as he opened the door, setting a bell jingling. "Unless you want to walk out the door with it."

He nodded, amused that she thought the warning necessary, and followed her into the shop.

SIX

Longstreet's Antiques always looked so crowded that Rachel thought Phil must use a shoehorn to fit everything in. When she'd said that to him, he'd laughed and told her that was one of the secrets of his business. When people saw the overwhelming display, they became convinced that they were going to find a hidden treasure and walk away with it for a pittance.

Even though she knew the motive behind it, the place exerted exactly that sort of appeal over her. She'd like to start burrowing through that box of odds and ends, just to see what was there. But she doubted that anyone ever got the better of Phil Longstreet on a deal. He was far too shrewd for that.

Thinking about bargains was certainly safer than letting her thoughts stray toward Tyler. She watched as he squatted beside a wooden box filled with old tools, face intent as he sifted through them. They'd gone so quickly to a level where she felt as if she'd known him for years instead of days.

But there was nothing normal about their friendship, if you could call it that. He'd come here for a purpose that involved her family, and she couldn't forget that. If anything he learned threatened her people—

He glanced up, catching her gaze, and smiled. A wave of warmth went through her. Maybe just for the moment she could shove other issues to the back of her mind and enjoy being with him.

"I'm ready for my lesson whenever you are, teacher." He stood, taking a step toward her.

Pennsylvania Dutch furniture, she reminded herself.

"Well, here's a good example of what's called a Dutch bench, which was on your list." She pointed to the black wooden bench with its decorative painting of hearts and tulips. "It's basically a love-seat-size bench with a back. It's a nice piece to use in a hallway."

He nodded, touching the smooth lacquer of the arm. "Now that I see it, I remember one like this. It was in the back hall. My grandfather used to sit there to pull his boots on before he went to the barn."

"It's not there now. I'd have noticed it when we were in the kitchen."

"No." He frowned. "Of course, it could have gone anytime in the past twenty years, and I wouldn't know the difference."

"A lot of small things might have disappeared without being noticed, even if the attorney visited the place occasionally. You should check on the dishes. According to the inventory, your grandfather had a set of spatterware."

His eyebrows lifted. "And I would recognize spatterware how?"

She glanced around, found a shelf filled with china, and lifted a plate down. "This is it. Fairly heavy, brightly painted tableware. Very typical of Pennsylvania Dutch ware."

Tyler bent over the plate, his hand brushing hers as he touched it. "So I'm looking for gaudy plates with chickens on them."

Laughter bubbled up. "I'll have you know that's not a chicken, it's a peafowl."

"I doubt any real bird would agree with that."

The amusement that filled his eyes sent another ripple of warmth through her. For a moment she didn't want to move. She just wanted to stand there with their hands touching and their gazes locked. His deep-blue eyes seemed to darken, and his fingers moved on hers.

She took a step back, her breathing uneven. It was some consolation that the breath he took was a bit ragged, as well.

"I…I should see where Phil has gotten to. Usually he comes right out when the bell rings." She walked quickly to the office door, gave a cursory knock and opened it. "Phil, are you in here?"

A quick glance told her he wasn't, but the door that led to the alley stood open, letting in a stream of cold air. She crossed to the door, hearing Tyler's footsteps behind her.

"Phil?"

A panel truck sat at the shop door, and two men were

loading a piece of furniture, carefully padded with quilted covers. Phil stood by, apparently to be sure they did it right. He looked toward her at the sound of her voice.

"Rachel, hello. I didn't hear you. And Mr. Dunn."

"Tyler, please." He was so close behind her that his breath stirred her hair when he spoke. And she shouldn't be so aware of that.

"I wanted to let you know we're here. I can see you're busy, so we'll look around." She glanced at the man lifting the furniture into the van, but his head was turned away as he concentrated on his work. Youngish, long hair—not anyone she recognized.

"Fine." Phil made shooing motions with his hands. "Go back in where it's warm. I'll be with you in a few minutes."

"Okay." Shivering a little, she hurried back to the showroom, relieved when Tyler closed the office door on the draft. "It's good that he's occupied. We can look at a few more things without listening to a sales pitch." She took the inventory from Tyler's hand. "Let's see what we can find."

By concentrating firmly on furniture, she filled the next few minutes with talk of dower chests, linen presses and pie cupboards, because if she didn't, she'd be too aware of the fact that Tyler stood next to her, looking at her as often as at the pieces of furniture she pointed out.

Finally the office door opened and Phil came in, rubbing his hands together briskly. "There, all finished at last. That lot is headed to a dealer in Pittsburgh."

"Do you have some new help?" she asked.

Phil shook his head. "Just a couple of guys I use some-times for deliveries. Now, what can I show you today?"

"How about showing me the brochure for the Christmas House Tour?"

"Now, Rachel, didn't I tell you I'd bring it over?"

"You did. You also said I'd have it yesterday."

She was vaguely aware of Tyler taking the inven-tory from her and sliding it into his pocket. Well, fair enough. She could understand his not wanting to share that information with anyone.

Phil threw his hands up in an exaggerated gesture. "Mea culpa. You're right, you're right, it's not finished yet."

"Phil, that's not fair." She didn't mind letting the ex-asperation show in her voice. This house tour had turned into a much bigger headache than she'd imagined. "You know that has to go to the printer, and the tour is coming up fast."

He stepped closer, reaching out as if he'd put his hand on her shoulder and then seeming to think better of it. "Forgive me, please? I know I promised, but you wouldn't believe how busy the shop has been lately."

"I'm happy for you. But the house tour is designed to help everyone's business, remember?"

"I'll finish it tonight and bring it to the inn first thing tomorrow morning. I promise. Forgive me?" He made a crossing-his-heart gesture, giving her the winsome smile that had persuaded too many elderly ladies to pay more than they'd intended.

She was immune. "Only if you don't let me down.

Tomorrow. By nine, so I can proof it and get it to the printer."

He sighed. "You're a hard woman. I'll do it, I promise. Now, did you come to buy or sell?" He looked expectantly at Tyler.

"Neither, I'm afraid. I just walked down with Rachel so I could have a look at your shop." Tyler smiled pleasantly. "Very impressive collection."

"Thank you, thank you. I'm always looking, you know. Any chance I might see what you have at the farmhouse soon?"

The police must not have been around. Surely he'd mention the break-in if he knew about it. She was relieved. Knowing Phil, an encounter with the police would probably throw him off his game so much that he'd be another week getting around to the brochure.

"I'll let you know." Tyler took a step toward the door.

"I'd be happy to do a free appraisal. Anytime." Phil retreated toward the counter. "I'll get right on the brochure, Rachel. You're going to love it."

"I'm sure I will." Aside from his propensity to put things off, Phil had a genuine artistic gift. Once he actually produced the brochure, it would be worth the wait.

She pulled the door open and nearly walked into Jeff Whitmoyer. They each stepped back at the same time, surprising her into a smile. "Come in, please. We were just on our way out."

"Morning, Rachel." His gaze went past her. "You must be Tyler Dunn. I've been wanting to talk to you."

Apparently they weren't getting out so quickly, after all. "Tyler, I'd like to introduce Jeff Whitmoyer. Jeff, Tyler Dunn."

Reminded of his manners, Jeff stuck his hand out, and Tyler shook it.

It was hard to believe Jeff and Bradley Whitmoyer were brothers—she thought that each time she saw one of them. Bradley was a lean, finely drawn intellectual with a social conscience that kept him serving his patients in this small community in spite of other, some would say better, opportunities.

Jeff was big, bluff, with a once-athletic frame now bulging out of the flannel shirt and frayed denim jacket he wore—certainly not because he couldn't afford better. He might not be the brightest bulb in the pack, as she'd heard Phil comment, but he made a good living with his construction company and was probably a lot smarter than people gave him credit for.

"Well, shut the door if you're going to talk." Phil's tone was waspish. "I'm paying the heating bill, remember?"

Jeff slammed the door, making the bell jingle so hard it threatened to pop off its bracket. "Wouldn't want you to spend an extra buck." He focused on Tyler. "I'd like to talk to you about the property of yours. I hear you're going to sell."

Tyler seemed to withdraw slightly. "Where did you hear that?"

Jeff shrugged massive shoulders. "Around. Anyway, I've had my eye on that place. I have some plans to develop that land, so how about we sit down and talk?"

Tact certainly wasn't Jeff's strong suit, but she supposed he'd think it a waste of time where business was concerned.

"I haven't reached that point yet, but thanks for your interest." Tyler reached for the door.

"Don't wait too long. I'll find something else if your place isn't for sale."

"Will you?" Phil's voice was soft, but Rachel thought she detected a malicious gleam in his eyes. "Given the scarcity of prime building land, I wonder where."

"Call me anytime. I'm in the book. Whitmoyer Construction." Jeff shook off Phil's needling like a bull shaking off a fly. "Talk to you soon."

Rachel waited until the door had closed behind them. Once they were well away from the shop, she spoke the thought in her mind. "You aren't seriously considering his offer, are you?"

"He didn't make an offer. But what's wrong with him? I thought those people were friends of yours."

"Nothing's wrong with him, except that I don't trust his taste. If he's talking about developing the land, he might have in mind a faux-Amish miniature golf course, for all I know."

His eyebrows lifted. "I should think a new attraction would draw more people. Isn't that what you want as a business owner?"

"Not something that turns the Amish into a freak show. Besides, our guests come to the inn for the peace and quiet of the countryside. How would you like your window to overlook a putting green or shooting range?"

"If and when I sell, I probably won't have much choice about what use the new owners make of the property. Any more than your neighbors could control your turning the mansion into a bed-and-breakfast."

He was being annoyingly rational, turning her argument against her in that way. She'd like to argue that at least her bed-and-breakfast, even if it benefited from its proximity to Amish farms, didn't make fun of them.

Maybe she shouldn't borrow trouble, but she couldn't help worrying how much Tyler's plans for the property were going to affect her future.

The strains of "Joy to the World" poured from the speakers of the CD player the next morning, filling the downstairs of the inn with anticipation. Rachel took a step back from the side table in the center hall to admire the arrangement of holly and evergreens she'd put in a pewter pitcher. The antique wooden horse toy next to it sported a red velvet bow around its neck.

"What do you think?" She turned to Grams and Emma, who were winding a string of greens on the newel post. "Should I add some bittersweet, too?"

"It looks perfect the way it is," Grams said. "I wouldn't change a thing."

Nodding, Rachel looked up at the molding along the ceiling, finding the eyehooks from which something could be hung. "Where's the Star of Bethlehem quilt? I'm ready to hang it now."

"The Star of Bethlehem quilt," Grams echoed. "I haven't seen it in ages."

Rachel blinked. "But we always hang it here. It's part of my earliest Christmas memories. We can't not have it." Absurd. She actually felt like bursting into tears.

Grams exchanged glances with Emma.

"I know chust where it is, *ja,*" Emma said quickly. "I will get it."

How silly she was, to be that obsessed with recreating the Christmases of her childhood. "You don't have to. If you'd rather put something else here—"

"Of course not," Grams said quickly.

"Well, let *me* get it, at least."

But Emma was already halfway up the stairs, her sturdy, dark-clad figure moving steadily. "It makes no trouble." S' disappeared around the bend in the stairs.

Gra.... led. "Don't worry about Emma. She enjoys the decorating as much as we do, even though it's not much of a tradition among the Amish."

"Not like you Moravians." Rachel smiled. "You're Christmas-decorating fanatics."

Grams's face went soft with reminiscence. "That's what it is when you grow up in Bethlehem. Every aspect of Christmas has its own tradition."

Grams had brought those traditions with her when she married. The Moravian star, the peppernuts, the *putz,* an elaborate crèche beneath the Christmas tree— those were part of the lovely Christmas lore she'd passed on to her granddaughters.

All Rachel's memories of Christmas had to do with Grams and Grandfather, not her parents. Hardly surprising, she supposed. Her parents had been separated so much of the time, with her father always off pursuing some get-rich-quick scheme or another. And her mom—well, Lily Unger Hampton had used the holidays as an excuse for extended visits to friends in the city. It had been Grams and Grandfather who made up Christmas lists, baked cookies, filled stockings.

Then Daddy had left for good and Mom had fought with Grandfather and taken the girls away. And their childhood ended.

She smiled at her grandmother, heart full. "We should go over to Bethlehem some evening while the decorations are still up. You know you'd love it."

"If we have time," Grams said, avoiding an answer. "We still have a lot to do before Christmas. I hope this weekend's guests don't mind our decorating around them."

"I'm sure they'll want to pitch right in." She hoped. Two couples would be arriving tomorrow, and there was no possibility she'd have everything finished by then. So her idea was to turn necessity into opportunity and invite the guests to join in.

"I hope so. They might be more enthusiastic than Tyler is, anyway." Grams looked a little miffed. She had suggested that Tyler might want to help them today, but he'd left the house early.

"Tyler's not in Churchville to enjoy himself, is he?"

Grams must have read something in her tone, because she gave her an inquiring look. "You're worried about that young man. I've told you—there's nothing he can find about your grandfather that will hurt us."

"I'm not worried so much about that as about what

he's going to do with the property. Jeff Whitmoyer approached him about buying it. Says he has plans to develop it."

"And you don't want that to happen?"

Rachel stared. "Grams, surely you don't want that either. He could put up something awful in full view of our upstairs windows. Fake Amish at its worst, if his other businesses are any indication."

"Oh, well, it won't bother us, and the Amish will ignore it as they do every other ridiculous thing that uses their name." Grams tweaked the ribbon on the newel post as Emma came down the stairs, the quilt folded over her arm.

Grams didn't seem too concerned, maybe because she didn't understand the possible effects. Their peaceful, pastoral setting was one of their biggest assets.

Emma unfurled the Star of Bethlehem quilt, and every other thought went right out of her mind. Here was the warmth of Christmas for her, stitched up in the handwork of some unknown ancestor.

Together she and Emma fastened the quilt to its dowel and climbed up to hang it in place. Once it was secure, she climbed back down and moved the stepstool away, then turned to look.

The star seemed to burst from the fabric, shouting its message of good news. Warmth blossomed through her. It was just as she remembered. After all those years of trekking around the country with her mother, with Christmas forgotten more often than not, the years when she'd been on her own, working on the holiday out of necessity, she'd longed for Christmas here.

Now she finally had it, and she wouldn't let it slip away. She had come home for Christmas.

"Ah, that looks lovely. I don't know why we ever stopped putting it up." Grams smiled. "This will be a Christmas to remember. You here to stay, Cal and Andrea coming home soon—if we could get Caroline to come back, it would be perfect."

Rachel hugged her. "We'll make it perfect, even if Caro doesn't come."

Grams patted her shoulder. "It's just too bad Tyler doesn't have any sense of belonging here. I'm afraid his grandfather and mother took that away from him a long time ago."

As was so often the case when it came to people, Grams had it right. Thanks to a family quarrel, Tyler had been robbed of that. Small wonder he didn't care who bought the land.

"His grandfather was a bitter man." Emma entered the conversation, planting her hands on her hips. "Turned against God and his neighbors when his wife died, left the church as if we were all to blame."

Rachel blinked. We? "Are you saying John Hostetler, Tyler's grandfather, was Amish?"

"*Ja,* of course." Emma's eyes widened. "Until he came under the *meidung* for his actions. You mean you didn't know that?"

The *meidung*—the shunning. The ultimate act for the Amish, to cut off the person completely unless and until the rebel repented. "How would I?" She turned to Grams. "You knew? But you didn't mention it to Tyler."

"Well, I just assumed he knew. Everyone in the area knew about it, of course. Do you mean he doesn't?"

She thought about their conversations and shook her head slowly. "I don't think so." Would it make a difference to him? To what he decided to do with the property?

She wasn't sure, but he should be told. And probably she was the one to tell him.

SEVEN

The office of the township police chief was tiny, with a detailed map of the township taking up most of one wall. Tyler sat in the sole visitor's chair, taking stock of his surroundings while he waited for Chief Burkhalter to return.

At a guess, the faded, framed photographs of past township events and the signed image of a former president were relics of the previous chief. He'd credit Zach Burkhalter with the up-to-date computer system and what seemed, looking at it upside down, to be a paperweight on the desk bearing the insignia of a military unit.

The door opened before he could follow the impulse to turn it around and take a closer look. Burkhalter came in, carrying a manila file folder and looking slightly apologetic.

"Sorry it took me so long to come up with this. My predecessor had his own method of filing that I still haven't quite figured out."

Tyler grasped the file, unable to suppress a sense of

optimism. If there was anything to learn about his grandfather's death, surely it would be here, in the police report.

He opened it to a discouragingly small sheaf of papers. "It looks as if he also didn't care to keep very complete records."

Burkhalter sat down behind his desk. "Things were pretty quiet around here twenty years ago. I don't suppose he'd ever had occasion before to investigate a case of murder."

Tyler shot him a glance. Burkhalter's lean, weathered face didn't give anything away. He couldn't be much older than Tyler himself, but he had the look of a man who'd spent most of those years dealing with human frailty in all its forms.

"Murder? I was afraid you wouldn't see it that way, since the death certificate says it was a heart attack that actually killed him."

The chief's eyes narrowed. "Heart attack or not, he died in the course of a crime, so that makes it murder in the eyes of the law. Since no one was ever charged, we don't know what a jury would have thought."

"That bothers you?"

"I don't like the fact that it was never solved." He looked, in fact, as if the case would have been worked considerably more thoroughly had he been the man in charge then.

Tyler flipped through the papers, seeing little that he hadn't already known. Apparently the crime had been discovered the next morning when a neighboring farmer noticed that the cows weren't out in their usual field. His interest sharpened at the name of the farmer. Elias Zook. A relative of the current Zook family, probably. He'd have to ask Rachel.

"The state police were called in," Burkhalter said. "I'll get in touch, see if they've kept the files."

"I'd appreciate it." He frowned down at a hand-written sheet of notes. "Apparently there were indications that more than one person was involved."

The chief nodded. "Hardly surprising, if they intended to rob him. Since I talked with you, I've looked through the records for that year. There were a number of robberies reported, isolated farms, owners elderly folks who sometimes couldn't even be sure when things went missing. Sort of like what's been happening recently."

"There've been other incidents of break-ins, then?"

Burkhalter's gray eyes looked bleak. "Several. Always isolated farmhouses, usually when no one was home. They're slick enough not to overdo it—might be a couple in a month, and then nothing for several months." His hand, resting on the desktop, tightened into a fist. "I'd like to lay my hands on them. Surprising, in a way, that they'd strike your place after you'd come back."

"Yes." He frowned. "I can't help but wonder if it had anything to do with the earlier crime, although I guess that's not very likely."

"No." But he detected a spark of interest in the chief's eyes. "If they thought they'd left any hint to their identity, they've had twenty years to take care of it."

"You think it's a coincidence, then."

Burkhalter considered for a moment. "Let's say I think it's a coincidence. But that I don't like coincidences."

It would not be a good idea to get on this man's bad side. Well, they both wanted the same thing, so that shouldn't be an issue.

He looked back down at the file. It contained a list of items that were presumed to have gone missing, the phrases so generic as to be useless. One side table. One rocking chair. He read a little farther. "There's mention here of a strong box that was found broken open and taken in for examination. No indication that it was ever returned to my mother. Any idea where that might be?"

Burkhalter held out his hand for the file, scanning it quickly. "If it didn't go back to the family, it's hard to tell. There are a few more files I can check. And the basement of this building is filled with all kinds of stuff that no one has ever properly documented. I'll have someone take a look around, but there's no guarantee we'll find it."

"I'd appreciate that." He rose. He'd been here long enough and found out very little. There wasn't much left to find after all this time. The sense of frustration was becoming familiar.

Burkhalter rose, too. "I'll let you know if we come up with anything. You're still at the inn?"

"Yes. I'm not leaving until I've disposed of the property. That's been left hanging for too long." Because his mother hadn't been able to forget how her father died, but she also hadn't known how to deal with it. Or hadn't wanted to.

"Folks will be glad to see that place taken care of." Burkhalter's eyes narrowed. "I just hope you're not planning to do any more police work on your own. If you know anything that might be helpful, even on a crime this old, you have a responsibility to divulge it."

Information? His mother's suspicions hardly fell into that category, and revealing them could harm innocent people.

"There's nothing, I'm afraid."

He had a feeling that Chief Burkhalter didn't entirely buy that, but he seemed to accept it for the moment.

"You'll let me know if anything occurs to you." It was more of an order than a request. "I'll be in touch if I find any reference to that strong box."

Tyler shook hands, thanking him, but without any degree of confidence that the strong box, or anything else, would appear. Everywhere he turned, it seemed all he found was another dead end.

Rachel tugged at the blue spruce she was trying to maneuver through the front door. Even with gloves on, the sharp needles pricked her, and as wide as the doorway was, it didn't seem—

"Having a problem?"

She'd seen Tyler pull in and had hoped she'd have the tree inside before he felt he had to come to the rescue. With the knowledge of his grandfather's Amish roots fresh in her mind, she'd have liked a little more time to decide how to approach the subject.

She managed a smile. "Large doorway, larger tree. It didn't look this big in the field."

"They never do." He replied easily enough, but she had the sense that some concern lurked.

Where had he been? She'd love to ask, but that would be prying.

"I seem to be stuck for the moment." She eyed the tree, halfway through the door. "I'm afraid you'll have to go around to the side."

"We can do better than that." He brushed past her, grasping the tree before she could caution him. "Ouch. You have one sharp Christmas tree."

She held up her hands, showing him the oversize gardening gloves she wore. "Blue spruce is my grandmother's favorite, and that's what I always remember being in the parlor when I was a child."

He paused in the act of pushing the tree through the door, turning to regard her gravely. "That's important to you, isn't it? Preserving the family traditions, that is."

Her throat tightened. If he knew a little more about her parents, he'd understand her longing to have the Christmas she remembered from her early childhood.

"I like family traditions." She could only hope she didn't sound defensive. "I just hope our guests will appreciate ours."

"It sounds as if you have plenty to choose from." With a final lift, he shoved the tree through into the entrance hall. Rachel followed quickly, closing the door against the chill air.

"True enough. Grams is of Moravian ancestry, and to them, celebrating Christmas properly is one of the most important parts of their heritage."

"What about the Amish?" He lifted the tree at the

bottom, seeming to assume he'd help her put it up. "Don't they have a lot of Christmas customs?"

The casual way he asked the question affirmed her belief that he didn't know about his grandfather's background. The need to tell him warred with her natural caution. What if she told him, and that knowledge influenced his decisions about the property in a negative way?

She grasped the upper part of the trunk and nodded toward the parlor, where the tree stand was ready. "The Amish, along with the other plain sects, don't do the type of decorating that the rest of the Pennsylvania Dutch do. Their celebration is focused on home and school. The children do a Christmas play that's a huge event for the Amish community."

He nodded, but again she had the sense that he was really thinking of something else.

"If I lift it into the stand, do you think you can steady it while I tighten the clamps?"

"You don't need to help, really." She shouldn't be relying on him, even for something as minor as this.

"I'm a better bet than enlisting your grandmother or the housekeeper." He hoisted the tree, lifting it into the stand.

"I'm sure you have other things to do." But she reached carefully through the branches to grasp the trunk where he indicated.

Tyler shed his jacket and got down on the floor, lying on his back to slide under the tree. The branches hid his face to some extent, and his voice sounded muffled.

"I've done all I can today, in any event. I had a talk with your police chief."

She wasn't sure how she felt about that, especially if he'd seen fit to tell Zach Burkhalter about his mother's suspicions.

"Was he helpful?" She hoped she sounded neutral.

She must not have succeeded, because Tyler slid out far enough to see her face.

"I didn't say anything about your family." He frowned. "He seems pretty shrewd. He probably knew I was holding something back."

"Yes, he is." Her thoughts flickered back to the problems they'd gone through in the spring. Burkhalter had suspected, correctly, that they'd been withholding information then. "Did he have anything you didn't already know?"

"He was open about sharing the files." Tyler's hands moved quickly, tightening the tree stand's clamps around the base of the spruce. It was a good thing. Her leg ached from the effort of holding the heavy tree upright.

"But…?"

"But apparently his predecessor wasn't very efficient. It looked to me as if he'd just gone through the motions of investigating."

"I'm sorry. I know how much that must frustrate you."

Tyler slid back out from under the tree, giving it a critical look. "Seems fairly straight to me. What do you think?"

She let go and stepped back. "Wonderful. Thank you so much." Her gaze met his. "Really, I'm sorry the chief wasn't able to help you."

He shrugged. "I didn't expect much, to be honest.

If there'd been anything obvious, the case would have been resolved a long time ago."

"I suppose so." But she knew he wasn't as resigned as he'd like to appear. He struck her as a man who succeeded at things that were important to him, and fulfilling a promise to his dying mother must be one of those.

The fact that his grandfather had been Amish didn't seem to relate at all, but how could she judge what might be important to him? She had to tell him, and now was as good a time as any.

She took a breath, inhaling the fresh aroma of the tree that already seemed to fill every corner of the room. "There is something that Grams mentioned to me. Something I think you ought to know, if you don't already."

He shot her a steely look, and she shook her head in response.

"I don't think it can have anything to do with his death. But did you know that your grandfather had been Amish?"

His blank stare answered that. "Amish? No. Are you sure? I don't remember seeing any Amish people at the funeral, and I'd have noticed something like that at that age."

"He'd left the church by then." She suspected he wouldn't be content with that.

"Left the church? You mean they shunned him?" His voice showed distaste. "They wouldn't even come to his funeral?"

She was probably doing this all wrong. "From what

Grams said, the choice was his, not theirs. Please don't think the Amish—"

"I don't think anything about them, one way or the other. Why should it matter to me? It's not as if my grandfather ever wanted a relationship with me. I'm doing this for my mother."

How much of his mother's personality had been determined by that bitter old man? Instinct told her Tyler needed to deal with those feelings, but she felt unable to reach him without crossing some barrier that would turn them into more than casual acquaintances.

"Families can be wonderful, but they can be hurtful, too." Like Daddy, leaving them without a goodbye. Or Mom, taking them away from the only security they'd ever known.

His hand came out and caught hers, holding it in a firm, warm grasp. "I guess you know something about it, don't you?"

"A bit. For me, my grandparents were the saving grace. I don't know who I'd be without them."

"My dad was the rock in our family. Anything I know about how to be a decent Christian man, I learned from him."

"You still miss him," she said softly, warmed by the grasp of his hand and the sense that he was willing to confide in her.

They had crossed that barrier, and it was a little scary on the other side.

He nodded. "He died when I was in my last year of high school, but I measure every decision against what I think he'd expect of me."

"If he knows, he must be glad that he had such an influence on your life."

"I hope he does." His voice had gone a little husky. He cleared his throat, probably embarrassed at showing so much emotion.

"You know," she said tentatively, "maybe knowing a little more about why your grandfather was the way he was would help you understand your mother, as well." She gave a rueful smile. "Believe me, if I could figure out what made my parents tick, I'd jump at the chance."

He seemed to become aware that he was still holding her hand, and he let go slowly. "I'll think about it. But there is something else you can do for me."

"Of course. What?"

"Your grandmother said you'd let me see your grandfather's ledgers. I'd appreciate that."

She felt as if someone had dropped an ice cube down her back. It took a moment to find her voice.

"Of course. I'll get them out for you." She turned away. She'd been wrong. They hadn't moved to a new relationship after all. Tyler still suspected her grandfather, and to him she was nothing but a source of information.

She had told Tyler she'd have the ledgers ready for him this evening, but that was beginning to look doubtful. Rachel looked up toward the ceiling of the church sanctuary, where a teenager perched at the top of a ladder, the end of a string of greenery in his hand. She was almost afraid to say something to him, for fear it would throw off his balance.

"That's fine, Jon. Just slip it over the hook and come back down."

He grinned, apparently perfectly at ease on his lofty perch. "Am I making you nervous, Ms. Rachel?"

"Definitely," she replied. "So get down here or I'll tell Pastor Greg on you."

Still grinning, he hooked the garland in place and started down, nimble as a monkey. She could breathe again.

She wasn't quite sure how she'd allowed herself to be talked into helping with the youth group's efforts to decorate the sanctuary for Advent. Supervising the teenagers' efforts might be harder than doing it herself, except that she'd never have gotten up on that ladder. The memory of flying off that stepladder when she'd put up the inn's Christmas lights was too fresh in her mind. She still didn't understand how that could have happened. How could she have missed something so obvious?

She moved back the center aisle, assessing their progress. In spite of a lot of horseplay and goofing off, the job was actually getting done. Swags of greenery cascaded down the cream-colored pillars that supported the roof, huge wreaths hung on either side of the chancel, and candleholders in each window had been trimmed with greenery. All that was left to do was to put new candles in all the holders.

She glanced at her watch. That was a good thing, since it was nearly nine, and she'd been told to send the kids off home promptly at nine.

"Okay, everyone, that's about it," she called above

the clatter of voices. "You've done a fantastic job. Just put the ladders away, please, and you'd better cut along home."

Jon Everhart paused, holding one end of the ladder. "Do you want me to stay and turn off the lights for you?"

"Thanks anyway, Jon. I'll do it. After all, I just have to walk across the street to get home."

Of course the kids didn't leave that promptly, but by ten after nine the last of them had gone out the walk through the cemetery to the street.

She picked up the box of new candles and started along the side of the sanctuary, setting them carefully in the holders. Maybe it was best that she do them herself in any event. Not that the kids hadn't done their best, but she'd feel better if she made sure the tapers were secure in the holders. On Christmas Eve every candle would be aflame, filling the sanctuary with light and warmth.

The sanctuary was quiet—quieter than she'd ever experienced. She seemed to feel that stillness seeping into her, gentling the worry that ate at her over the problem presented by Tyler and her continuing anxiety about the financial state of the inn.

She looked at the window above her, showing Jesus talking with the woman at the well. His face, even represented in stained glass, showed so much love and acceptance. In spite of her tiredness, she felt that caring touch her, renewing her.

I've come so close to You since the accident. Maybe the person who hit me actually did me a favor. He couldn't have intended it, but the accident forced me to stop running away spiritually.

She knew why she'd done that, of course. She spent years unable to refer to God as Father, until she'd finally realized that it made her think of her own father, absent most of the time and fighting with Mom when he was around.

Tyler had his own issues with his parents, but at least he'd had a positive relationship with his father for most of his young life. Did he realize how fortunate he was in that? Or was he too wrapped up in his inability to satisfy his mother's demands?

She started down the opposite side of the sanctuary, securing candles in holders. She should finish this up and get back to the inn. It wasn't really all that late. She could still locate the pertinent ledgers and turn them over to Tyler. Let him strain his vision all he wanted, reading through her grandfather's meticulous notes. He wouldn't find anything to reflect badly on Grandfather, no matter how hard he looked.

She was putting the last candle in place when the lights went out. A startled gasp escaped her. She froze, feeling as if she'd suddenly gone blind.

Slowly her vision adjusted. The faintest light filtered through the windows, probably from the street-lamp at the gate to the churchyard. Dark shadows fell across the sanctuary, though, and if she tried to cut across to where she knew the light switches were, she'd probably crash right into a pew.

Here she stood with a box full of candles and not a single match to light one. The sensible thing was to feel her way along the wall until she got to the front pew where she'd left her handbag. The small flashlight she kept in her bag would help her reach the light switches.

Running her left hand along the cool plaster, reaching out with her right hand to touch the pews, she worked her way toward the front of the sanctuary. Why would the lights go out, anyway? It wasn't as if they were in the midst of a lightning storm.

Still, Grams had often said that the church building, just about as old as the inn, had similar problems. Maybe the overloaded circuits had chosen this moment to break down.

Or the explanation might be simpler. Mose Stetler, the custodian, could have come in, thinking they'd all left, and switched the lights off.

She paused, one hand resting on the curved back of a pew, its worn wood satiny to the touch. "Mose? Is that you? I'm still in the sanctuary."

Really, he should have checked to see if anyone was here before going around switching off lights.

No one answered. If it was Mose, he apparently couldn't hear her.

She took another step and stopped, her heart lurching into overdrive. Someone was in the sanctuary with her.

Ridiculous. She was being foolish, imagining things because she was alone in the dark. She took another step. And heard it. A step that echoed her own and then stopped.

She should call out. It must be someone on a perfectly innocent errand—Mose, or even the pastor, come to see that the church had been properly locked up. She should call out, let them know she was there.

But some instinct held her throat in a vise. She couldn't—she really couldn't speak. Stupid as it seemed, she was unable to make a sound.

Or was it so stupid? She'd already called out, and no one had answered. Whoever was there, he or she seemed anxious not to be heard or identified.

She drew in a cautious breath, trying to keep it silent. Think. A chill of fear trickled down her spine. She'd become disoriented in the dark. How far was she from the double doors at the rear of the sanctuary? How far from the chancel door that led out past the organ to the vestry?

Her fingers tightened on the pew back, and she strained to see. Directly opposite her there was a faint gleam coming through the stained glass. Surely that was the image of Jesus with the woman at the well, wasn't it? She could just make out the shape of the figure.

All right. Be calm. If that window was opposite, then she was nearer to the chancel door, wasn't she?

She took a cautious step in that direction, then another, gaining a little confidence. She didn't know where the other person was in the dark, but if she could make it to the door and get through, she could close it. Lock it. She tried to form an image of the door. Lots of the sturdy old wooden doors in the church had dead bolts. Did that one?

She wasn't sure. But she'd still feel a lot better with

a closed door between her and the unknown person. She could move quickly through the small vestry, and beyond it was the door that led out to the ramp. It had a clear glass window, so she'd be able to see to get out.

She took another step, groping for the next pew, and froze, her breath catching. A footstep, nearer to her than she'd thought. He was between her and the chancel door—a thicker blackness than the dark around him. Did he realize how close they were? Surely he couldn't see her any better than she could him. If he did, a few steps would close the gap between them.

Not daring to breathe, she inched her way backward, moving toward the outer wall this time. Follow the wall back to the rear of the sanctuary, work her way to the door.

Please, Lord, please. Maybe I'm being silly, but I don't think so. I think there's danger in this place. Help me.

A few silent steps, and her hand brushed the wall. Holding her breath, she moved along it. She'd be okay, she'd reach the back of the church—and then she realized that the footsteps were moving toward her, deliberately, no longer trying to hide.

How did he know—stupid, she was silhouetted against the faint light coming through the stained glass. Moving to the outer wall was the worst thing she could have done. Heedless of the noise, she dove into the sheltering blackness of the nearest pew, sensing the movement toward her of that other, hearing the indrawn breath of annoyance.

Her heart thudded so loudly she could hear it, and

terror clutched her throat. She couldn't stay here, helpless in the dark, waiting for him to find her. Even as she formed the thought she heard him move, heard a hand brushing against the pew back, groping.

She scuttled toward the center aisle, praying he couldn't tell exactly which row she was in. If he came after her—yes, he was coming, she couldn't stop, she didn't dare hesitate—

She bolted along the row, giving up any idea of silence. Her knee banged painfully against the pew and then she was out, into the aisle, sensing the clear space around her.

No time to feel her way. She ran toward the back, a breathless prayer crying from her very soul. *Help me, help me.*

Running full tilt, she hit the door at the rear of the sanctuary. It exploded open, and she bolted out into the cold night, less black than the sanctuary had been. She flew down the few stairs and ran into a solid shape, heard a gasp and felt hard hands grab her painfully tight.

EIGHT

Tyler wrapped his arms around Rachel, feeling her slender body shake against him. The grip of her hands was frantic, her breath ragged.

"Rachel, what's wrong?" He drew her close, all the exasperation he'd been feeling gone in an instant. "Are you hurt?"

She shook her head, but her grip didn't loosen, and he found her tension driving his own.

"Come on, Rachel. You're scaring me. Tell me what's wrong." He tried to say it lightly, but the depth of concern he felt startled and dismayed him. When had he started caring so much about Rachel?

She took a deep breath, and he felt her drawing on some reserve of strength to compose herself. "Sorry. I'm sorry." She drew back a little. "I'm not hurt. Just scared."

"Why? What scared you?" Fear spiked, making his voice sharp.

She pushed soft brown curls away from her face with a hand that wasn't entirely steady.

"The lights went out. I was in the sanctuary, finishing up the decorating by myself, when the lights suddenly went out."

"There's more to it than that." He gripped her shoulders. "You wouldn't panic just because you were alone in the dark."

She shook her head. "That's just it. I wasn't alone." She drew in a ragged breath. "Someone was there. I know how stupid that sounds, but someone was in there with me."

The fear in her voice made him take it seriously. "Did someone touch you—say something to you?" His mind jumped to the dark figure who'd struck him down at the old farmhouse. But the two things couldn't be related, could they?

She seemed to be steadying herself, as if talking about it was relieving her fear. "I heard him. Or her. I couldn't be sure. And I saw—well, just a shadow."

He studied her face, frowning a little. He didn't doubt what she was saying, but it was hard to imagine a threat against her in the church.

"You don't believe me." Her chin came up.

"I believe you." He ran his hands down her arms. "I'll go in and have a look around." He hefted the torch Rachel's grandmother had given him when he'd said he'd come over to the church and walk her back.

"Not without me." Her fingers closed around his wrist. "Come around to the side. We can go through the education wing door and get to the light switches from there."

If someone was hiding in the sanctuary, that would give the person a chance to escape while they were going around the building. "Maybe we should call the police."

She hesitated, and he could almost see her weighing the possibilities. Finally she shook her head. "I guess it's not a crime to turn off the lights, is it? Let's see what we can find."

He nodded and let her lead him along the walk. Once they'd rounded the corner, they could see the lamp above the side door shining. "Looks like the power's still on in this wing. Could be only one circuit was shut off."

Rachel marched to the door and turned the knob. It wasn't locked. "This is the way we came in. I was supposed to lock it with the key when I left. The sanctuary doors are locked, but they open from the inside."

A good thing, given the way she'd erupted through them. He followed her inside. She reached out, flipping a switch, and lights came on down a hallway with what were probably classrooms on either side.

"Everything seems okay here."

She nodded. "The door to the vestry is around the corner at the end of the hall."

He started down the hallway, not attempting to be quiet. His footsteps would echo on the tile floor, in any event.

Rachel walked in step with him, her face intent but pale, her hands clenched. Obviously she was convinced that something malicious had been intended in the incident. He still wasn't so sure, but—

Footsteps. Someone was coming toward them,

around the corner. He heard the quick intake of Rachel's breath. His hand tightened on the flashlight. He grasped Rachel's arm, pushing her behind him.

A figure came around the corner, and all of his tension fell flat. The man had to be eighty at least, and he peered at them through the thick lenses of his glasses.

"Rachel?" His voice quavered. "That you?"

"Mose." Relief flooded Rachel's voice. "I'm glad to see you."

He grunted. "Pastor told me you'd be hanging the greens in the sanctuary tonight. You all finished?"

"Yes, we're done. Why didn't you answer me when I called to you in the sanctuary?"

The old man blinked several times before replying. "In the sanctuary? Haven't been in the sanctuary yet. Just came in the side door and was on my way here when I heard you folks come in." He glanced at Tyler suspiciously.

The color she'd regained melted from Rachel's face. "You weren't? But someone was. The lights went off."

"Lights off?" He sniffed. "We'll just see about that." He turned and shuffled off the way he'd come.

They followed him, and Tyler realized that at some point he'd grasped Rachel's hand. Well, she was scared. Giving her a little support was the least he could do.

Around the corner, through a set of double fire doors, and they were abruptly in the old part of the building again. In the dark. He switched on his flashlight, and the old man's face looked white and startled in its glare.

"Must be a circuit. Just shine your light over to the right, so's I can see what's what."

Tyler did as he was told and the flashlight's beam picked out the gray metal circuit box, looking incongruous against a carved oak cabinet that must be at least a hundred years old.

The custodian flipped it open. "There's the problem, all right. Breaker's thrown." He clicked it, and lights came on immediately, gleaming through an open door that led into the sanctuary.

"Let's have a look inside." Tyler moved to the door. "Rachel heard someone in there."

The elderly man followed them into the sanctuary. The lights showed evergreen branches looping around the columns and flowing around the windows. Everything looked perfectly normal.

Rachel stood close to him. "I'd like to walk back through, just to be sure."

He nodded, sensing that she didn't want to say anything else within earshot of the custodian.

Halfway back along the outside wall, she stopped. "This is where I was," she murmured. "When I realized he was coming toward me. I ducked into that pew, ran along it and out the center aisle to the doors."

"He didn't follow you then?"

"I'm not sure. I was pretty panicked by then. All I wanted was to get out."

Hearing a faint tremor in her voice, he found her hand and squeezed it. "You're okay now."

She nodded, sending him a cautioning look as the custodian came toward them.

"Well, if someone was here, they're gone now." He patted Rachel's arm. "Don't like to say it, but most likely it was one of them kids. Their idea of a joke."

"I guess it could have been." Rachel sounded unconvinced. "Thanks, Mose. Do you want me to go back through and turn off the lights?"

"No, no, you folks go on. I'm going that way anyhow."

Touching Rachel's arm, Tyler guided her toward the door, still not sure what he thought of all this. That Rachel had been frightened by someone, he had no doubt. But was it anything more than that?

They walked side by side out into the chilly night and along the walk. He waited for Rachel to speak first. Their relationship was fragile at best, and he wasn't sure what he could say to make this better.

They reached the street before she spoke. She glanced at him, her face pale in the gleam of the streetlamp. "I suppose Mose could be right about the kids. Though I hate to think they'd be so mean."

He took her hand as they crossed the street toward the inn. "Kids don't always think through the results of their actions. I can remember a couple of really stupid things I did at that age."

She smiled faintly. "I suppose I can, too. Well, thank you for coming to the rescue. I hope I didn't look like too much of an idiot."

"You didn't look like an idiot at all." His fingers tightened on hers. "It was a scary experience, even if

Mose is right and it was just intended as a joke. I'm just not sure—" He hesitated. Maybe he shouldn't voice the thought in his mind.

"What?" They neared the side door, and she stopped just short of the circle of illumination from the overhead light.

"I've only known you…what? A week? In that time you've been nearly electrocuted by Christmas lights and—well, call it harassed in the church."

Her face was a pale oval in the dim light. "And you've been hit on the head."

"Seems like we're both having a run of bad luck." He waited for her response.

She frowned, looking troubled. "It does seem odd. But the Christmas lights—surely no one could have done that deliberately."

"Not if they didn't have access to them. If they were safely up in your attic until the moment you brought them down to hang—"

"They weren't," she said shortly. "I brought them down the day before. I was checking on them when I realized it was time for the committee meeting."

He didn't think he liked that. "Where were they during the meeting?"

"In the downstairs rest room."

"Where someone could tamper with them," he said.

"Why would anyone do that? They're all my friends. Anyway, how could they have known I'd be the one to put them up?"

"Anyone who's been around the inn would know that."

She took a quick step away from him, into the pool of light. "I can't believe that someone I know would try to hurt me." But her voice seemed to wobble on the words.

"I'm not trying to upset you." An unexpected, and unwelcome, flood of protectiveness swept through him. "I'm just concerned."

"Thank you. But please, I don't want Grams to know anything happened. She worries about me."

"She loves you," he said quietly, prompted by some instinct he wasn't sure he understood. "That's a good thing."

She tilted her face back, a smile lifting the corners of her lips. "Most of the time," she agreed.

"All of the time." Without thinking it through, he brushed a strand of hair back from her face. It flowed through his fingers like silk.

Her eyes widened. Darkened. He heard the faint catch of her breath. Knew that his own breathing was suddenly ragged.

He took her shoulders, drawing her toward him. She came willingly, lifting her face. The faintest shadow of caution touched his mind, and he censored it. His lips found hers.

Astonishing, the flood of warmth and tenderness that went through him. The kiss was gentle, tentative, as if Rachel were asking silently, Is this right? Do we want to do this? Who are you, deep inside where it's important?

She drew back a little at last, a smile lingering on her lips. "Maybe we'd better go in."

He dropped a light kiss on her nose. "Maybe we'd better. Your grandmother will be worrying."

But he didn't want to. He wanted to stay out here in the moonlight with her as long as he could. And he didn't care to explore what that meant about the state of his feelings.

Barney trotted along Crossings Road next to Rachel, darting away from her from time to time to investigate an interesting clump of dried weeds or the trunk of a hemlock. She smiled at his enthusiasm, aware that they were coming closer to the farm with every step.

And that Tyler was there. She'd really had no intention of coming back here or seeing Tyler this afternoon. But Grams had said Rachel was driving them crazy tinkering with the Christmas decorations, and that everything was as ready as it could be for the guests who'd be arriving late this afternoon. Why didn't she take Barney for a walk and get rid of her fidgets?

The dog, apparently remembering their last excursion, had promptly led her down Crossings Road to the Hostetler farm. They reached the lane, and Barney darted ahead of her. She could see Tyler's car, pulled up next to the porch. He'd told Grams he was trying to identify the rest of the furniture today.

To say that she had mixed feelings about seeing Tyler was putting it mildly. She'd appreciated his help the previous night. He'd managed to submerge whatever doubts he had about her story and given her the help she needed.

As for what had happened—she stared absently at the clumps of dried Queen Anne's lace in what had once been a pasture.

Surely she could think about it rationally now. Little though she wanted to believe it, Mose's suggestion was the only sensible one. One or more of the teenagers, motivated by who knew what, could easily have flipped the switch to turn the lights off. Maybe they'd thought it would be funny to give her a scare in the dark.

Well, if so, she'd certainly gratified them by bolting out the way she had. She should have turned the tables on them and grabbed that person in the sanctuary.

She couldn't have. Cold seemed to settle into her. Even now, in the clear light of day with the thin winter sun on her face, she couldn't imagine reaching out toward that faceless figure.

Her steps slowed, and Barney scampered over to nose at her hand. She patted him absently.

Maybe it had been her imagination. She sincerely hoped it had been. But that sense of enmity she'd felt, there in the dark in what should have been the safest of places, had simply overpowered her. She'd reacted like any hunted animal. Run. Hide.

She forced her feet to move again. Just thinking about it was making her feel the fear again, and she wouldn't let fear control her.

Remembering what had happened afterward was disturbing in a different way. She couldn't stop the smile that curved her lips when she remembered that kiss. It had held a potential that warmed her and startled her. It certainly hadn't clarified things between them—if anything, she felt more confused.

And then what he'd suggested about the Christmas lights—well, it couldn't be, that was all. Except that his words had roused that niggling little doubt she'd felt every time she looked at the lights.

And he was right. Anyone who was there that night could have guessed she'd put them up. It would have been the work of a minute to strip the wires.

Not a surefire way of hurting her, but a quick and easy impulse.

Tyler had left someone out, though. Himself.

He'd had access to the lights, too. And he'd come here convinced that her family was guilty of something in relation to his grandfather's death.

Was he really just after the truth? Or did revenge figure in somewhere?

Ridiculous, she told herself firmly. He wasn't that sort of devious person.

But still—maybe that was all the more reason not to see Tyler alone today. She'd reached the house, but he wasn't inside. Instead she spotted him where the ground sloped up behind the barn.

For a moment she didn't know what he was doing, but then she realized. That tangle of brush and rusted fence was a small cemetery, of course. There were plenty of them, scattered throughout the township, most of them remnants of the earliest days of settlement. Some were well kept, others abandoned. This one fell into the abandoned category.

Tyler seemed totally absorbed. He hadn't noticed her. Good. She'd turn around and go back to the inn—

But before she could move, Barney spotted Tyler and plunged toward him, tail waving, letting out a series of welcoming barks. Tyler looked up and waved. Nothing for it now but to go forward.

Tyler climbed over the remnants of the low wrought-iron fence and stood, waiting for her. Barney reached him first, and Tyler welcomed him, running his hand along the dog's back and sending Barney into excited whines.

"Hi." He surveyed her, as if measuring the amount of strain on her face. "How are you doing? I wondered when I didn't see you at breakfast."

"I'm fine," she said quickly. "Just fine. Grams thought I could use a sleep-in day before the weekend guests get here, that's all."

He nodded, as if accepting that implication that she didn't want to discuss the previous night.

"How did you make out with the furniture?" she asked quickly. "Grams said you were trying to get through the list today."

"I managed to do that, but I'm not sure how far ahead it gets me. There are certainly plenty of things missing, and I can make up a list to give the chief. But there's no way of knowing when anything disappeared. My grandfather could have sold some of it himself, for all I know."

She could understand his frustration. He was finding dead ends everywhere he turned.

"So you're investigating the family cemetery, instead."

Get 2 Books FREE!

Steeple Hill Books,
publisher of inspirational fiction, presents

Love Inspired
SUSPENSE

A SERIES OF EDGE-OF-YOUR-SEAT SUSPENSE NOVELS

FREE BOOKS!
Get two free books by acclaimed, inspirational authors!

FREE GIFTS!
Get two exciting surprise gifts absolutely free!

To get your 2 free books and 2 free gifts, affix this peel-off sticker to the reply card and mail it today!

GET 2 FREE BOOKS!

HURRY!

Return this card promptly to get **2 FREE Books** and **2 FREE Bonus Gifts!**

Love Inspired.
SUSPENSE

YES! *Please send me the 2 FREE Love Inspired® Suspense books and 2 FREE gifts for which I qualify. I understand that I am under no obligation to purchase anything further, as explained on the back of this card.*

affix
free
books
sticker
here

323 IDL EL4Z   123 IDL EL3Z

FIRST NAME	LAST NAME

ADDRESS

APT.#	CITY

STATE/PROV.	ZIP/POSTAL CODE

◀ **DETACH AND MAIL CARD TODAY!** ▼

Steeple Hill Reader Service™—Here's How It Works:

Accepting your 2 free books and 2 free gifts places you under no obligation to buy anything. You may keep the books and gifts and return the shipping statement marked "cancel." If you do not cancel, about a month later we will send you 4 additional books and bill you just $3.99 each in the U.S. or $4.74 each in Canada, plus 25¢ shipping & handling per book and applicable taxes if any.* That's the complete price, and — compared to cover prices of $4.99 each in the U.S. and $5.99 each in Canada — it's quite a bargain! You may cancel at any time, but if you choose to continue, every month we'll send you 4 more books, which you may either purchase at the discount price...or return to us and cancel your subscription.

*Terms and prices subject to change without notice. Sales tax applicable in N.Y. Canadian residents will be charged applicable provincial taxes and GST. All orders subject to approval. Books received may not be as shown. Credit or debit balances in a customer's account(s) may be offset by any other outstanding balance owed by or to the customer. Please allow 4 to 6 weeks for delivery.

"Not so much family, as far as I can tell. Most of the people buried here seem to be Chadwicks, dating back to the 1700s."

"The land probably originally belonged to a family called Chadwick. Once it came into Amish hands, they'd have been buried in the Amish cemetery over toward Burkville."

He knelt, straightening a small stone that had been tipped over. "Miranda Chadwick. Looks as if she was only three when she died."

She squatted next to him, heart clenching, and shoved a clump of soil against the marker to hold it upright. "So many children didn't survive the first few years then. It's hardly surprising that people had big families." She touched the rough-cut cross on the marker, unaccountably hurt by the centuries-old loss. "They grieved for her."

He nodded, his face solemn, and then rose, holding out his hand to help her to her feet.

She stood, disentangling her hand quickly, afraid of what she might give away if she held on to him any longer.

He cleared his throat. "So you said the Amish are buried elsewhere?"

"The Amish have a church-district cemetery—at least, that's how it's done here. Just simple stones, most of them alike, I guess showing that even in death, everyone is equal."

"But my grandfather had left the church by the time he died." Something sharp and alert focused Tyler's gray eyes. "So where would he be buried?"

"I don't know. Maybe my grandmother—"

But Tyler was already moving purposely through the small graveyard, bending to pull the weeds away from each stone. Feeling helpless, she followed him.

Chadwicks and more Chadwicks. Surely he wasn't—

But Tyler had stopped before one stone, carefully clearing the debris from it, and she realized the marker looked newer than the others.

Why this sudden feeling of dismay? She struggled with her own emotions. It didn't really make a difference, did it, where Tyler's grandfather was buried?

She came to a stop next to him, looking at Tyler rather than the stone. His face had tightened, becoming all sharp planes and angles.

"Here it is. John Hostetler. Just his name and the dates. I guess my mother held to Amish tradition in that, at least."

She couldn't tell what he was feeling. She rested her hand lightly on his shoulder. Tension, that was all she could be sure of. She focused on the marker.

John Hostetler. As Tyler said, just date of birth. Date of death.

Date of death. For an instant her vision seemed to blur. She shook her head, forcing her gaze to the carved date. It was like being struck in the stomach. She actually stumbled back a step, gasping.

Tyler was on it in an instant, of course. He shot to his feet, grasping her hands in both of his. "What is it?"

She shook her head, trying to come up with something, anything other than the truth.

Tyler's grip tightened painfully. He couldn't have

known how hard he was holding her. "What, Rachel? What do you see when you look at the tombstone?"

She couldn't lie. Couldn't evade. Couldn't even understand it herself.

"The date. The date your grandfather died." She stopped, feeling as if the words choked her. "My father deserted us at just about the same time."

NINE

Tyler could only stare at Rachel for a moment, questions battering at his mind. He reached out, wanting to hold her so that she couldn't escape until he had all the answers. How could she land a blow like that and then stand looking at him as if it didn't matter?

Then he realized that it wasn't lack of caring that froze her face and darkened her eyes. Shock. Rachel was shocked by this, just as he was.

A cold breeze hit them, rustling the bare branches of the oak tree that sheltered the few tilted gravestones. Rachel shivered, her whole body seeming to tremble for a moment.

He grasped her arm. "Come on. Let's get back to the car and warm up."

She walked with him down the hill, stumbling a little once or twice as if not watching where she was going. Barney, darting around them in circles in the frostbitten field, seemed to sense that something was wrong. He rushed up to Rachel with small, reassuring yips.

They reached the car. He tucked her into the passenger seat and started the ignition, turning the heater on. Barney whined until he opened the back door so the dog could jump in.

Tyler slid into the driver's seat, holding out his hand to the vent, grateful for the power of the car's heater. Already warmth was coming out, and he turned the blower to full blast. He couldn't possibly get any answers until Rachel lost that frozen look.

For several minutes she didn't move. He should take her back to the inn, but he'd never have a better time than this to find answers.

She stretched her hands out toward the heater vent, rubbing them together, and the movement encouraged him. She seemed to have lost a little of that frozen look.

"Feeling better now?" He kept his voice low.

She nodded, darting a cautious, sideways glance at him. To his relief the color had returned to her cheeks.

"I'm sorry. I don't know what got into me."

"Shock," he suggested.

"I don't—" She stopped, shook her head, made an effort to start again. "I'm being stupid, letting the coincidence upset me so much."

He discovered his hand was gripping the steering wheel so hard the knuckles were white, and he forced his fingers to loosen.

"Do you really think it's a coincidence that your father deserted you about the time of my grandfather's death?"

"What else could it be?" Defiance colored the words.

Plenty of things, most notably a guilty conscience.

But he suspected she would come to that conclusion on her own if he didn't push too hard.

She moved, as if the silence disturbed her. "I was only eight. I might be remembering incorrectly." Her voice was so defensive that he knew there was more to it than that.

"You must know around when it was. Didn't you tell me that your mother took you and your sisters away shortly after that?"

Her mouth was set, but she gave a short nod.

"Kids usually have their own ways of remembering when things happened. Connecting the experiences to being off school or holidays or—"

He stopped, because a tremor had shot through her, so fierce he could feel it. He reached out, capturing her cold hand in his. "What is it, Rachel? You may as well tell me, because you know I'm not going to give up."

She stared through the windshield at the bleak landscape. Barney whined from the backseat, seeming to sense her distress.

"My birthday would have been a week after your grandfather's death." The words came out slow. Reluctant. "I was excited because Daddy had promised to stay for my birthday and give me a gold cross necklace, like the one Andrea had." She seemed to be looking back over a dark, painful chasm. "But he was gone before then."

"Promised to stay? You mean he wasn't usually there?"

"Our parents were separated so much it's hard to keep track. Daddy would be gone for months at a time, and then show up. He and Mom might get along for a few weeks, then something would blow up between them and he'd leave." She threaded her fingers through her hair. "Not the most stable of parents. I sometimes wonder why they had us."

He willed himself to go slow, to think this through. Hampton had deserted his family at about the time of his grandfather's death; that was clear. But connecting the two incidents with any sureness was iffy, given what Rachel said about her father's absences.

"Had your dad been around much that summer?"

She frowned, shaking her head. "I'm not sure. It seems to me that he had, but—" She shrugged. "He could be so charming, although I don't think my grandparents saw it. Life seemed exciting when he was here."

She'd wanted to be loved, of course. Any child knows instinctively that a parent's love is crucial.

"Do you remember anything about when your dad left?" He tried to keep his voice gentle.

She stared down at her hands. He sensed that she was pulling her defenses up, figuring out how to cope with this situation.

"I don't know much." Her voice was calmer now, as if she were able to detach her grown-up self from the little girl who'd been looking forward to her birthday. "I'm sure the adults were all trying to protect us, but of course Andrea and I speculated. We crept out on the stairs at night. I remember sitting there, holding her hand, listening to my mother shouting at my grandparents, as if it was their fault he'd gone."

Her fingers twisted a little in remembered pain, and he smoothed them gently, hurting for her.

"Your mother must have explained things to you in some way."

A wry smile tugged at her lips. "You didn't know our mother if you think that. She just announced that Daddy was gone and that we were going away, too. She hauled us out of the house with half our belongings. For a while Drea and I thought we were going to join our father, but that didn't happen. Every time we asked, she'd tell us to be quiet." She shrugged. "So finally we stopped asking."

He struggled to piece it together. It sounded as if her family had been far more messed up than his. "So your parents never got back together?"

She shook her head. "Being taken away from our grandparents hurt the worst. Daddy had been in and out of our lives so much, always trying some great new job that was going to make all the difference. It never did."

"So your grandparents were the stable influence." And probably only her grandmother, or possibly Emma, could tell him the story from an adult perspective.

"They were. If Mom had let us see them more often—but she nursed her own grudge against them. It really wasn't until we were in college that we had much contact with them. Still, we always knew they were there." She brushed back a strand of silky hair, managing to give him something approaching a normal smile. "When I came back a year ago, just for a visit, I realized this place was what I'd been longing for all along. It's home, even though I left it when I was eight."

He nodded, understanding. Wanting to make it better for her, even at the same time that he knew he'd have to find out more about her father.

He touched the strand of hair she fiddled with, tucking it behind her ear. His fingers brushed her cheek, setting up a wave of longing that he had to fight.

"I'd have to say you turned out pretty well, in spite of your parents. What happened to them? Are you still in contact?"

She shook her head. "Mom died in a car accident three years ago in Nevada."

"I'm sorry." Although it didn't sound as if she'd been much of a loss as a mother. "What about your dad?" Casual. Keep it casual.

She blinked. "I thought you realized. We haven't heard a word from him from that day to this."

Maybe the worst thing about running an inn was the fact that no matter what was going on in her personal life, Rachel had to be smiling and welcoming for the guests. She could only be thankful that at the moment, Grams had their weekend guests corralled in the front parlor, serving them eggnog and cookies and regaling them with Pennsylvania Dutch Christmas legends, while Rachel had the back parlor to herself, getting the nativity scene ready to go beneath the Christmas tree.

If only she'd had a little more self-control, Tyler

would never have known about the coincidence in dates between her father's leaving and his grandfather's death. That was all it had been. A coincidence. She'd never believe that her feckless, generous father could have been involved in that. Never.

She frowned at the low wooden platform that was meant to hold the *putz*. That end didn't seem to be sitting properly.

Keeping her hands busy unfortunately allowed her mind to wander too much.

I guess I couldn't have kept it from Tyler, could I? She had a wistful longing that God would come down on her side in this, but in her heart she knew it wouldn't happen. "Be ye wise as serpents and innocent as doves." Hiding the truth from Tyler was hardly an act of innocence.

Still, the fear existed. What would he do with the information he now had? She already knew part of that answer, didn't she? He'd want to talk to Grams. She hadn't remembered much about that time, but Grams would.

All her protective family instincts went into high gear at the thought, but there was nothing she could do. Tyler wouldn't be deflected, and Grams would do what was right.

Having arranged the molds to hold the hills and valleys on the wooden platform, she spread out the length of green cloth that was meant to cover them. The fabric fell in graceful folds, looking for all the world like real hills and valleys.

And then the end of the platform collapsed,

sending her neat little world atilt. For a moment she felt like bursting into tears. Her world really was falling around her, and there seemed to be nothing she could do to stop it.

"Looks as if you need a carpenter."

Her heart jolted at the sound of Tyler's voice. She didn't look up. "My brother-in-law is a carpenter, but he moved his shop to the property he and Andrea bought in New Holland. And he's off on his honeymoon, anyway."

Tyler knelt beside her, his arm brushing hers as he righted the platform. She caught the tang of his aftershave and resisted the instinct to lean a little closer to him.

"I think I can manage to fix this. Will you hand me that hammer?"

She passed it over to him. With a few quick blows he firmed up the nails that had begun to work themselves loose.

She caught his sideways, questioning glance, as if he wanted to ask how she was but was afraid to start something.

"This is the foundation for the nativity scene, I take it."

"We call it the *putz*." She spread the cloth out again, aware of his hands helping her. "If you want to hear about it, you should go to the front parlor. Grams is giving the details to the other guests."

Was that ungracious? Grams would certainly think so.

"I'd rather hear it from you." Tyler's voice was low, pitched under the chatter from the other room.

"That's not what you want, and you know it." She couldn't seem to help the tartness in her tone.

Tyler nodded, blue eyes serious as he studied her face. "All right. That's true. You realize I have to talk to your grandmother, don't you?"

She paused in the act of removing one of the clay nativity figures from its nest of tissue paper. Even without seeing it, she could identify the shape of a camel through the paper.

She'd been anticipating this moment—getting out the familiar old figures, setting up the scene until it was just perfect. Irrational or not, she couldn't help but resent the fact that Tyler was spoiling it for her.

"I know you need to hear the story from Grams." Her words felt as fragile as the crystal ornaments on the tree. "I'd appreciate it if you'd wait until we've gotten through this evening."

"I'll wait, but later we have to talk." The implacability in his tone chilled her. He wouldn't be turned back, no matter what.

Even if what he was trying to do implicated her father.

"And now we're ready to set up the *putz*, or nativity scene." Grams came through the archway, shepherding the four new couples firmly. "We hope you'll enjoy doing this traditional Pennsylvania German tradition with us."

Both mother-daughter pairs looked enthusiastic. The other two couples were from Connecticut. The women seemed pleased, the men bored. How long before they made some excuse to get out of this? They looked slightly heartened at the sight of Tyler— another male to support them, she supposed.

But Tyler would want to get this over as quickly as possible, so he would corner Grams.

"You've already met my granddaughter Rachel when you checked in." Grams performed introductions. "And this is our friend, Tyler Dunn."

How did Tyler feel about being promoted from guest to friend? It wouldn't stop him from finding out all he could about her father.

While Grams explained the tradition of the *putz*, the elaborate Nativity scene that went under the tree, Rachel unwrapped the six-inch clay figures, setting them out on the folding table she'd brought in for the purpose.

"...not just a manger scene," Grams explained. "We start at the left and create little vignettes of the events leading up to the birth of Jesus—Joseph in his carpentry shop, Mary with the angel, the trip to Bethlehem. The stable scene goes front and center, of course, and then the shepherds with their flocks, the wise men following the star, even the flight to Egypt."

"These are beautiful figures." One of the women grabbed an angel, holding it up in one hand.

Rachel had to force herself not to take it back. That was the angel with the broken wing tip. She'd knocked it over the year she was six and been inconsolable until Daddy, there for once, had touched it up with gilt paint, assuring her that no one would ever notice.

"Antique," Tyler said smoothly, "and very fragile. Difficult to replace."

The woman seemed to take the hint, holding the angel carefully in both hands. "We actually get to help set this up? Well, if that isn't the sweetest thing."

She knelt by the platform. The others, seeming infected by her enthusiasm, gathered around to take the delicate figures or the stones and moss Rachel had brought in to add realism to the scene. In a few moments everyone was happily involved. Tyler even enlisted the two men to create a miniature mountain, and she thought she caught a serious discussion about how one might add a running stream.

She stood back a little, watching the scene take shape, handing out a figure where needed. Funny, how sharp the memory had been when she'd seen the angel with the chipped wing. She hadn't thought of that in years.

Maybe it had been so strong because it involved her father. Funny. You'd have expected the oldest daughter to be Daddy's girl, but instead it had been her. The whole time they'd lived here, everyone had known that Andrea was Grandfather's little helper and she was Daddy's girl.

Was it because Andrea was less guided by sentiment? A little more clear-sighted about their parents? The thought made her uncomfortable, and she tried to push it away.

"Rachel?"

She blinked, realizing that one of the guests must have said her name several times. "Yes? Peggy," she added, pleased to have pulled the woman's name from her memory banks.

"Will you show me how to put these Roman soldiers together? It looks as if the shield should hook on, but I don't quite see…"

"Let me." Tyler took it from the woman. She looked up at him, obviously flattered at his attention. "I think we can figure this out together, can't we?"

The woman fluttered after him in an instant, kneeling at the base of the tree next to him.

Rachel pinned a smile to her face. She couldn't let her private worries distract her from her duty to her guests. But Tyler—

Tyler had been watchful. Sensitive. Seeming to know what she was feeling, quick and subtle about helping out.

Even as she thought that, she caught him taking a clay donkey from Grams and handing her a star to be nestled in the branches instead, so that she didn't attempt to get down on the floor.

The simple gesture gripped her heart. Without warning, the thought came. This was a man she could love.

No. She couldn't. Because whether he wanted to or not, Tyler threatened everything that was important to her.

Rachel clearly didn't intend to let him talk to her grandmother tonight. The other guests had lingered long after the Nativity scene was finished. As it happened, one of the women was an accomplished pianist, and she'd entertained them with Christmas music while a fire roared in the fireplace and tree lights shone softly on the *putz*.

It was lovely. He'd had to admit that—admit, too, that he'd enjoyed watching the firelight play on Rachel's expressive face.

Too expressive. She probably didn't realize how clearly her protectiveness toward her grandmother came through. Once the last of the guests had wound down, she'd put her arm around the elderly woman's waist and urged her toward the stairs with a defiant look at him.

Well, much as he needed to talk to Katherine Unger, he had to agree with Rachel on this one. She had looked tired, and it was late. Tomorrow would have to do.

He put the book he'd been leafing through back on the shelf and headed for the stairs. As he did, the door into the private wing of the house opened. It wasn't Rachel who came through—it was her grandmother.

"Mrs. Unger." He stopped, foot on the bottom step. "I thought you'd already gone to bed."

"That's what my granddaughter thinks, too." She stepped into the hall, the dog padding softly behind her, and closed the door. "I think it's time we had a talk about whatever it is you and Rachel have been trying to keep from me all day."

"I'm not sure—"

She took his arm and steered him back down the hall toward the kitchen. "My granddaughter is too protective. Now, don't you start, too. Whatever it is won't be improved by making me wait and wonder about it until morning."

A low light had been left on in the kitchen, shining down on the sturdy wooden table that had undoubtedly served generations of the family, and a Black Forest clock ticked steadily on the mantelpiece. Mrs. Unger sat at the table and gestured him to the chair next to her.

"Now. Tell me." She folded thin, aristocratic hands in a gesture that was probably her way of armoring herself against bad news. "You and Rachel learned something today that upset her. What was it?"

He hesitated. "I don't think Rachel is going to like my talking with you alone."

"I'll deal with Rachel." She waited.

"All right." Actually, this might bother her less than it did Rachel. "I was in the small cemetery at the farm today. The one where my grandfather is buried. Rachel saw the date he died. I think you know why that upset her."

Her face tightened slightly at the implied challenge, but she nodded. "It reminded Rachel of when her father left."

"That's what she said." He frowned, trying to find the right way to ask questions that were certainly prying into her family's affairs. "She didn't remember the sequence of events exactly. Maybe she didn't even know, at the time."

"But you knew I would." She said the words he'd omitted, shaking her head as if she didn't want to remember. "That was a difficult time. Rachel's father had been around for nearly a month—long for him. The quarrels were starting up. We knew it was only a question of time until he left. The fact that it happened shortly after your grandfather's death doesn't mean they were related."

"Perhaps not. But you must know I won't be satisfied unless I get some answers."

She inclined her head, conceding the point. "You

have that right, I suppose." A faint, wry smile flickered. "Oddly enough, I've waited for years for Rachel
to ask the questions. Why did her father leave? Why
did their mother take them away? She never has."

That was strange. He'd think the questions would
burn in her. "I don't want to hurt her. Or you. But I
need the truth."

"The truth always costs something. Probably pain."
She held up her hand to stop his protest. "I'm not
refusing to tell you. I'm just pointing out that you
can't always protect people." She sighed, her fingers
tightening against each other. "Maybe that was my
mistake. Trying to protect everyone."

Yes, he could see that. She was someone who
would always try to protect her family. Rachel was
exactly the same. As much as it might annoy him at
times, he had to admire it, too.

"We only had the one child, you know." Her voice
was soft. "Perhaps things would have been different
if we'd had more. As it was, Lily was the apple of her
father's eye—spirited, willful and headstrong. My
husband liked those qualities in her, until she met
Donald Hampton."

"He didn't approve." He'd only had Rachel's child's-
eye view of her father, but he hadn't been too impressed.

"No. Oh, Hampton was charming. Good-looking,
polite. It was easy to see why she fell in love with him.
But Frederick didn't think there was much character
behind the charm."

His mind flickered to his own father. Maybe not

long on charm, but he'd been a sound man and a good
father. Odd, to be sitting in this quiet room with this
elderly woman, pulled willy-nilly into a bond with
her.

She sighed, the sound a soft counterpoint to the
ticking of the clock. "Frederick would have stopped
the marriage if he could have, but she was determined.
And afterward there were the babies—" Her face
bloomed with love. "He adored those girls. Hampton
was just as unreliable as my husband predicted, but
Frederick managed to keep his opinions to himself, for
the most part. And we were happy when they moved
in here. Then it didn't matter when Hampton took off,
supposedly in search of some wonderful deal. We
could take care of the children."

It seemed to him that their mother should have done
that, but apparently she hadn't, from what Rachel said,
been especially gifted as a mother.

"They were living here when my grandfather was
attacked." Maybe best to move things along.

"Yes. As I said, Hampton had been back for about a
month, supposedly trying to find a decent job around
here, although Frederick always said he would run at the
sight of one. Still, he was here, and Rachel adored him."

He'd seen that, in her eyes, when she spoke of him.
"Maybe that's why she's never asked. She wants to
hold on to her image of him."

She nodded. "We thought he'd be here until
Rachel's birthday, at least."

"How long after the attack on my grandfather did
he leave?" That was the important point to him.

"Two days." Her face tightened until the skin seemed molded against the bone. "We woke up to find him gone. He left a note, telling Lily he'd heard of some wonderful job opportunity out west. He left, never even saying goodbye to the girls. I don't think they ever heard from him again."

The timing was certainly suspicious. "I understand your daughter left soon after that."

"There was a terrible quarrel between them—my daughter and my husband. Frederick was rash enough to say what he thought of her husband, never imagining she'd carry out her threat to leave." She shook her head, the grief she'd probably carried since that day seeming to weigh her down. "I tried to reason with them, but they were both too stubborn to listen. There was a time when I thought I'd never get my granddaughters back again."

"But you have," he said quickly. "They never stopped loving you." Love. Connections. They went together, didn't they? Binding people together for good or ill. Like it or not, his family and hers were bound, too.

"I do." She looked at him then, and he saw the pleading in her lined face. "I have Rachel, and through her Andrea came back, too. But Rachel is the vulnerable one. She always has been. Family is everything to her."

What could he say to that? She didn't seem to expect anything. She just leaned across the table, putting her hand over his.

"Please," she said. "Please don't do anything that will take family away from Rachel. Please."

TEN

Rachel charged up the stairs the next morning, fueled by a mix of rage and betrayal. Tyler had gone too far this time.

Imagine the nerve—he'd sat there at breakfast calmly eating her cream-cheese-filled French toast, listening to the other guests talk about their planned day in Bethlehem, and he hadn't shown her by word or look that he had talked to Grams last night.

Some latent, fair part of her mind suggested that he could hardly have brought up something so personal in the presence of strangers, but she slapped it down. She wasn't rational about this. She was furious.

She paused on the landing, catching her breath, calming her nerves. Her sensitivity where her father was concerned was probably getting in the way of her judgment, but she couldn't seem to help it.

If only Andrea were here. She knew her big sister well enough to know that if she called Andrea's cell phone and told her what was going on, she and Cal would be on their way home immediately. But that wasn't fair—not to Andrea, who deserved to have her honeymoon in peace, and not to herself. It was time she stopped depending on her big sister.

She went quickly up the rest of the flight, running her hand along the carved railing. The square, spacious upstairs hall looked odd with the bedroom doors closed. All of their guests had gone out for the day. Except Tyler.

She swung on her heel toward his door just as it opened.

"Rachel." His face changed at the sight of her.

Small wonder. She probably looked like an avenging fury. She certainly felt like one.

"We have to talk." She said the words with control, but her nails were biting into her palms.

He nodded, opening the door wide. "I know. Do you want to come in?"

Instinct told her not to have this conversation in the privacy of the bedroom. "Out here is fine. Everyone's left. We won't be overheard." No matter what she had to say to him.

"Right." He stepped out into the hallway, closing the door behind him, and just stood, waiting for her to say what she would.

All the insults she'd been practicing in her head seemed to fly away at the sight of his grave face. She could only find one thing to say.

"How could you? How could you talk to my grandmother without me?" Saying the words seemed to give her momentum. "You must have known how tired she was and how much that was bound to upset her. I can't believe you'd do that."

It was true, she realized. At some level, she couldn't believe that the Tyler she'd grown to know and care for would go behind her back that way.

"If you've talked with your grandmother, you know I didn't go to her," he said calmly. "She came to me."

"Yes. I know. I also know that you could have made some excuse. You could have waited until today at least. Why was it so important that you had to talk about it last night? Grams—" To her horror, she felt tears welling in her eyes. She blinked them back.

But he saw. He took a step toward her, closing the gap between them, his face gentling.

"Don't, Rachel. Please. I don't want to hurt you. I didn't want to hurt her. But your grandmother is one smart lady. She knew we were hiding something from her, and she wasn't going to rest until she knew what it was."

She drew in a breath, trying to ease the tension in her throat. "She is smart. And stubborn."

His fingers closed over hers for a brief moment. "Like her granddaughter."

Another breath, another effort to gain control of the situation that seemed to be slipping rapidly away from her. Or maybe there had never been anything she could do about this, but it had taken her this long to realize it.

"Grams told me what she'd told you. About my father leaving, the fight between my grandfather and mother." She shook her head slightly, not liking the pictures that had taken up residence there. "She's convinced that his leaving didn't have anything to do with what happened to your grandfather." She forced herself to meet his eyes.

"So am I. Maybe he was just as charming as I remember and just as weak as my grandparents thought, but he wasn't a man who'd turn to violence."

"I hope you're right, Rachel." His fingers brushed hers again in mute sympathy. "I hope you're right about him."

She nodded, throat clogging so that she had to clear it. Unshed tears would do that to a person. "Well. I guess I'm not angry enough to slug you after all."

His smile was tentative, as if he were afraid of setting her off again. "I'm sure there are things for which I deserve it, anyway, so feel free."

Her tension drained away at the offer. "Not today. Grams said I should thank you for bringing it out in the open—about my father leaving, I mean. I'm not quite ready to do that."

"Not necessary," he said quickly. "I know things I have no right to about your family. And you about mine. Neither of us can do anything about it."

He was right about that. She didn't have to like it, but she had to accept it. He probably felt the same way.

"I am grateful for your help last night with the guests." She managed a smile that was a bit more genuine. "You really picked up the slack for me."

He shrugged, seeming to relax, as well. "My pleasure. I have to hand it to you and your grandmother. You certainly have a hit on your hands with the Pennsylvania Dutch Christmas traditions. Those people will tell their friends, and before you know it, every room will be full for the holidays."

"I just hope everything will go more easily once

we've had a little practice." Realizing how close they were standing, she took a step back, bumping into the slant-top desk that stood between the doors.

"Easy." He reached out to steady her and then seemed to change his mind about touching her again and put his hand on the satiny old wood instead. "Don't want to harm either you or this beautiful thing."

"I'm not sure which is more valuable." She straightened the small vase of bittersweet that stood on the narrow top.

"You are," he said, and then nodded toward the desk. "But that is a nice piece. I remember something like it in my grandfather's house." He frowned, and she thought memory flickered in those deep-blue eyes.

"What is it?"

He shook his head. "Funny. I guess being here has brought back more memories. It's as if a door popped open in my mind. I can actually picture that desk now. It used to stand in the upstairs hall." He shook his head. "I'm sure it wasn't a beautiful heirloom like this one, though."

The air had been sucked out of the hall, and she was choking. She couldn't say anything—she could only force a meaningless smile.

The slant-top desk wasn't the family heirloom he obviously supposed it to be. She'd found the piece stuffed away in one of the sheds and refinished it herself when she was getting the inn ready to open.

Coincidence, she insisted. It had to be. The desk was a common style, and surely plenty of homes in the area had one like it.

"Rachel?" Tyler stared at her, eyes questioning. "Is something wrong?"

"No, not at all." She had a feeling her attempt at a smile was ghastly. "Nothing—"

She broke off at the sound of footsteps coming up the stairs. Sturdy footsteps that could only belong to Emma.

Emma rounded the turn at the landing, saw them, and came forward steadily. Rachel glanced at Tyler. He might not have noticed it, but Emma had been doing a good job of avoiding speaking with him. Now, it appeared, she was headed straight for him.

Emma came to a halt a few feet from them, her face square and determined, graying hair drawn back under her white kapp.

"I would like to speak with Tyler Dunn, *ja?*" She made it a question.

"Of course." Rachel took a step back. "Do you want to be private?"

"No, no, you stay, Rachel." She looked steadily at Tyler. "Mrs. Unger tells us that you are John Hostetler's grandson. That you might want to know about him. My Eli's mother, she minds him well. You come to supper Monday night, she will be there, tell you about him, *ja?*"

Tyler sent her a quick glance, as if asking for help. She tried not to respond. She'd already let herself get too involved in Tyler's search for answers, and look where it had gotten her. She'd been leading the trail right where she didn't want it—back to her own family.

"That's very kind of you, Mrs. Zook." Tyler had apparently decided she wasn't going to jump in. "I appreciate it."

Emma gave a short, characteristic nod. "Is *gut*. Rachel, you will come, too. That will make it more easy."

Not waiting for an answer, Emma turned and started back down the stairs, the long skirt of her dark-green dress swishing.

Rachel opened her mouth to protest and closed it again. Emma was bracketing her with Tyler, apparently assuming that she was helping him in his search. But Emma didn't know everything. Rachel carefully avoided glancing at the desk. She'd think that through later. In the meantime—

"Look, I'll understand if you don't want to go with me," Tyler began.

"No. That's fine. I'll be happy to go."

Well, maybe "happy" was a slight exaggeration. But like it or not, she seemed to be running out of choices. The circle was closing tighter and tighter around her family.

Staying close to Tyler was dangerous, but not knowing what he was doing, what he was finding out—that could be more dangerous still.

Rachel tried to focus on Pastor Greg's sermon, not on the fact that Tyler Dunn was sitting next to her in the small sanctuary. She'd resigned herself to the necessity of working with Tyler. She just hadn't expected that cooperation to extend to worshipping next to him.

Sunday morning with guests in the house was always a difficult time. She'd served breakfast, hoping she wasn't rushing anyone, and then scrambled into her clothes.

When she'd rushed out to meet Grams in the center hallway, Tyler had been there, wearing a gray suit tailored to perfection across his broad shoulders, obviously bound for church as well. They could hardly avoid inviting him to accompany them.

She took a deep breath, trying to focus her mind and heart. Unfortunately the heady scent of pine boughs sent her mind surging back to the night she'd faced fear in this place.

And Tyler had been there to help her. She stole a glance at him. His strong-boned face was grave and attentive. He didn't seem to be experiencing any of the distraction she felt.

Maybe he had better forces of concentration than she did. That was probably important to an architect. She wasn't doing as well. Because of the trouble he'd brought into their lives, still unresolved? Or whether because of the man himself?

She folded her hands, fingers squeezing tight, and emulated Grams, serenely focused on the pastor's sermon.

Grams would show that same attention and respect no matter who was in the pulpit. She hoped she would, as well, but Pastor Greg always gave her some sturdy spiritual food to chew on.

Today the topic was angels—not fluffy, sentimental Victorian Christmas card angels, but the angels of the Bible. Grave messengers from God, exultant rejoicers at Jesus's birth. Her wayward imagination caught, she listened intently, rose to sing the closing hymn and floated out of the sanctuary at last on a thunderous organ blast of "Angels We Have Heard on High."

The spiritual lift lasted until she reached the churchyard, where Sandra Whitmoyer grabbed her arm. "Rachel, I must speak with you about the open house tour."

Of course she had to. Rachel stepped out of the flow of exiting parishioners, buttoning her coat against the December chill.

"I thought we were all set. You received the brochures, didn't you?" Phillip had finally responded to her prodding and produced a beautiful brochure, which she'd dutifully delivered to the printer.

"Yes, yes, the brochures are fine." Sandra tucked a creamy fold of cashmere scarf inside the lapel of her leather coat. "But Margaret Allen wants to serve chocolates along with her other refreshments at The Willows. Now, you know we can't risk having people put sticky, chocolaty hands on antique furniture when they go on to the next house."

"It will be all adults on the tour," she pointed out. "I'm sure they'll be responsible about touching things."

Besides, she had no desire to take on the owner of a competing bed-and-breakfast. They'd had their run-ins with Margaret in the past, and she didn't want to reopen hostilities.

"You don't know that," Sandra said darkly. "Some people will do anything. I won't have people touching the Italian tapestry on my sitting room love seat with sticky fingers."

Sandra was caught between a rock and a hard place, Rachel realized. She'd been the first to offer her lovely old Victorian home for the tour, but she'd been worrying ever since that some harm would come to her delicate furnishings.

"If I might make a suggestion—" Tyler's voice was diffident. She might have forgotten that he was standing next to her, he'd been so quiet, but she hadn't.

Sandra gave him a swift smile instead of the argumentative frown she'd been bestowing on Rachel. "Of course. Any and all suggestions are welcome."

Especially when they came from an attractive male. Rachel chastised herself for her catty thoughts. And practically on the doorstep of the church, no less.

"You might have each stop on the tour offer a container of hand wipes at the entrance. It's only sensible during cold and flu season, in any event."

"Brilliant." Sandra's smile blazed. "I don't know why I didn't think of that myself. Or why my husband didn't suggest it—"

"Didn't suggest what?" Bradley Whitmoyer slipped his arm into the crook of his wife's arm.

While Sandra was explaining, Rachel took another quick glance at Tyler's face. Could he possibly be interested in all this? His gaze crossed hers, and her heart jolted.

He looked so serious. Worry gnawed at her. If he'd found out about the desk—

But that was ridiculous. How could he? He'd hardly

go around asking Grams or Emma about the provenance of a piece of furniture.

She'd asked both of them herself, cautiously, if they
knew where the piece had come from. Emma had
shaken her head; Grams had said vaguely that perhaps
Grandfather had bought it at an auction.

Impossible to tell. The outbuildings were stuffed
with furniture. Andrea had been after her to have a
proper inventory made, but who had time for that?

Maybe she should be up-front with Tyler about the
desk. After all, even if it had come from his grandfather's farm, that meant nothing. He could have sold it—

She was rationalizing, and she knew it. She didn't
want to tell him because it was one more thing to make
him suspect her father. First her grandfather, now her
father. Where was it going to end?

She forced her attention back to the conversation in
time to find that Tyler's suggestion had been adopted and
that Sandra, thank goodness, would take care of it herself.

"I think we've kept these people standing in the
cold long enough." Bradley nudged his wife toward
the churchyard gate.

He was the one who looked cold. Maybe it went
along with being overworked, which he probably was
now that flu season had started.

Rachel turned away, feeling Tyler move beside her.
She probably should have suggested that he go on
back to the inn—after all, none of this would matter
to him. But before they'd gone more than a couple of
yards, Jeff Whitmoyer stepped into their path, his face
ruddy from the nip in the air.

"Hey, glad I ran into you, Dunn." He thrust his hand toward Tyler. "You have a chance to give any thought to my offer? I'd like to get my plans made, be able to break ground as soon as the ground thaws in the spring."

"I don't recall your saying what you planned for the property, if you should buy it." Tyler sounded polite but noncommittal.

Jeff glanced from one side to the other, as if checking for anyone listening in. "Let's say I have an idea for an Amish tourist attraction and leave it at that. When can we sit down and talk it over?"

"Not today," Tyler said. "I don't do business on Sunday."

Before Jeff could suggest another day, Rachel broke in. "Speaking of work to be done in the spring, Jeff, I'd like to get on your work schedule to get that gazebo in the garden moved."

"Moved?" Jeff looked startled. "Who told you that thing could be moved?"

"I did," Tyler said smoothly.

"Tyler is an architect," Rachel added. "He suggested moving the gazebo to the far side of the pond, and I'd like to do that. If you can handle it."

"Of course I can handle it," Jeff said, affronted. "I just don't see why you'd want to move it. I thought you told me last spring you wanted it torn down. Still, if that's what you and your grandmother want, I'll get it on my schedule. I'll stop by and take a look at it this week—maybe talk to you at the same time, Dunn."

Tyler gave a quick nod and took her arm. "We'd better get your grandmother back to the house." He steered her toward Grams, who broke off a conversation with one of the neighbors when she saw them.

Well, she'd gotten Tyler away from Jeff Whitmoyer for the moment, but she didn't know what good that had done. Sooner or later Tyler would settle for whatever truth he found about his grandfather. He'd sell the property and go back to his own life. He probably wouldn't care what use was made of the property after that.

They'd reached the curb when one more interruption intercepted them, in the shape of the police cruiser, pulling to the curb next to them. Chief Burkhalter lowered the window and leaned out.

"Some information for you, Dunn." He shook a keen, assessing glance toward her and Grams. "That lockbox we were talking about—it's turned up. You can stop by my office tomorrow, if you want, and pick it up."

"Thanks. I'll do that."

She caught the suppressed excitement in Tyler's voice, and tension tightened inside her. Box? What box? He hadn't mentioned this to her. She wasn't the only person keeping secrets, it seemed.

"I hope you don't mind driving over to the Zook farm." Rachel glanced at him as he held the door of his car for her, her soft brown curls tumbling from under the knitted cap she wore. "It's an easy walk from the path beyond the barn, but not in the dark. I'd hate to have you arrive with burrs on your pant legs."

"That wouldn't look too good, would it? Am I appropriately dressed?" He hadn't known what the Amish would consider decent attire for an outsider supper guest, so he'd settled on gray flannels and a sweater over a dress shirt.

"You're fine." She pulled her seat belt across. "One thing about the Amish—they don't judge outsiders by what they wear."

How did they judge, then? He closed Rachel's door, walked around the car and slid in. He wasn't nervous—the fact that his grandfather, even his mother, apparently, had been Amish was curious, that was all.

Rachel glanced at him as he started the car. "Relax. They'll be welcoming, I promise."

He turned out onto Main Street. "It's odd, that's all. If not for my grandfather's break with the church, my life might have turned out differently."

He stopped. Impossible to think of himself being Amish. Tonight's visit was going to be meaningless, but he'd hardly been able to refuse Emma's invitation.

Rachel seemed content with the silence between them as he drove past the decorated houses and shops. Or was *content* the right word? He'd sensed some reservation in her in the past day, and he wasn't sure what that meant.

"Looks as if your Christmas in Churchville committee is doing a good job. The only thing missing to turn the village into a Christmas card scene is a couple of inches of snow."

"It does look lovely, doesn't it?" The eagerness in her voice dissipated whatever reserve he'd been imagining. "This is exactly how I've pictured it. Like coming home for Christmas. Don't you think?"

It wasn't the home he'd known, but he understood. "That's it. You'll send visitors away feeling they have to come back every year for their Christmas to be complete."

He understood more than that. That her pleasure and satisfaction was more than just the sense of a job well done. It was personal, not professional. Rachel had found her place in the world when she'd come back here.

It wasn't his place, he reminded himself. His partner was already getting antsy, e-mailing him to ask how soon he'd be coming back.

He deserved the time off, he'd pointed out to Gil. And it certainly wasn't a question of Gil needing him in the office. They had a good partnership, with Gil Anders being the outgoing people-person while he preferred to work alone with his computer and his blueprints.

Baltimore is not that far away, a small voice pointed out in the back of his mind. It would be possible to come back. To see Rachel again.

Always assuming Rachel wanted to see him once this whole affair had ended.

Rachel leaned forward, pointing. "There's the lane to the Zook farm."

He turned. "The Christmas lights seem to stop here."

"No electricity." He sensed Rachel's smile, even in the dark. "The Amish don't go in for big displays, in any event. Christmas is a religious celebration. The day after, the twenty-sixth, they call 'second Christmas.' That's the day for visiting and celebrating."

He nodded, concentrating on the narrow farm lane in the headlight beams. "You certainly have a lot of different Christmas traditions going in this small area. I like your grandmother's Moravian customs."

"You'd see even more of that if you went to Lititz or Bethlehem. That reminds me, I want to run over to Bethlehem sometime this week to take more photos and pick up a stack of brochures before the next weekend guests come in."

The farmhouse appeared as they passed a windbreak of evergreens, lights glowing yellow from the windows.

"Just pull up by the porch," Rachel instructed. "The children are already peeking out the windows, watching for us."

While he parked and rounded the car to join Rachel, he went over in his mind what she'd told him about the family. Emma and Eli, her husband, now lived in a kind of grandparent cottage, attached to the main house, while their son Samuel and his wife, Nancy, ran the farm with their children. There was another son, Levi, who was mentally handicapped. Nobody seemed to be considered too young, too old or too disabled to contribute to the family, as far as he could tell from what Rachel had said.

The front door was thrown open as they mounted the porch, and they were greeted by five children—blond stair steps with round blue eyes and huge smiles. The smallest one, a girl, flung herself at Rachel for a hug.

"You're here at last! We've been waiting and waiting. Maam says that you might hear me do my piece for the Christmas program. Will you, Rachel?"

Rachel tugged on a blond braid gently. "I would love to hear you, Elizabeth. Now just let us greet everyone."

The adults were already coming into the room. In rapid succession he was introduced to Eli, their son Samuel, and his wife, Nancy, a brisk, cheerful woman who seemed to run her household with firm command. If he'd imagined that Amish women were meek and subservient, she dispelled that idea.

"This is my mother, Liva Zook." Eli held the arm of an elderly woman, her hair glistening white, her eyes still intensely blue behind her wire-rimmed glasses. "She will be glad to talk with you about your grandfather."

He extended his hand and then hesitated, not sure if that was proper. But she shook hands, hers dry and firm in his.

"You sit here and talk." Nancy ushered him and Eli's mother to a pair of wooden rockers.

He nodded, waiting for the elderly woman to sit down first and then taking his place next to her. The room initially seemed bare to his eyes, but the chair was surprisingly comfortable, the back of it curved to fit his body and the arms worn smooth to the hand.

Eli pulled up a straight chair and sat down next to his mother. "Maam sometimes does not do well in English, so I'll help." He reached out to pat his mother's hand, and Tyler could see the bond between them. Eli's ruddy face above the white beard had the same bone structure, the same round blue eyes.

He'd begun to get used to the Amish custom of

beards without mustaches, and the bare faces with the fringe of beard no longer looked odd to him.

"Thanks." Now that he had the opportunity, he wasn't sure how to begin. "If you could just tell me what you remember about my grandfather—"

For a moment he was afraid she didn't understand, but then she nodded. "I remember John. We were children together, *ja*." She nodded again in what seemed a characteristic gesture.

"What was he like?" Was he ever different from the angry, bitter man who had turned everyone away from him?

She studied his face. "Looked something like you, when he was young. Strong, like you. He knew his mind, did what he wanted."

He glanced from her to Eli. "The Amish church doesn't like that, does it?"

"He was young." Her lips creased in an indulgent smile. "The young, they have to see the other side of the fence sometimes."

"Rumspringa," Eli said. "Our youth have time to see the world before they decide to join the church. So they know what they are doing." His eyes twinkled. "Some have a wilder *rumspringa* than others."

Sensible, he thought. It surprised him, in a way, that the Amish would allow that. They must have a lot of confidence that their kids wouldn't be lured away by the world.

"*Ja*, that was John Hostetler. Always questioning. Always wanting to know things not taught in our school. Folk worried about him." She frowned slightly, folding her hands together on the dark apron she wore. "But then he began courting Anna Schmidt. They had eyes for no one else, those two."

It was odd, he supposed, that he hadn't even thought about his grandmother. "I never knew her."

"She died when her daughter was only twelve." Her eyes clouded with sympathy. "Your maam, that was."

"What was she like? My grandmother?"

Pert and lively like young Elizabeth, who was bouncing up and down as she recited something for Rachel on the other side of the room? Nurturing, like Emma, or brisk and take-charge, like Nancy?

"Sweet-natured. Kind." The old woman smiled, reminiscing. "She was very loving, was Anna. Seemed as if that rubbed off on John when they married. But when she died—" She shook her head. "He turned against everyone. Even God."

Something in him rebelled at that. "Maybe if people had tried to help him, it would have been different."

"We tried." Tears filled her eyes. "For Anna, for himself, for the community. Nothing did any good. He would not listen. He turned against everything Anna was." She shook her head. "She would have been so sad. You understand. She was one who couldn't stop loving and caring."

He nodded, touched by the image of the grandmother who'd barely entered his mind before this. Someone sweet. Loving. Dedicated to family.

He glanced across the room at Rachel, her face lit with laughter as she hugged the little girl.

Like Rachel. Loving. Nurturing. Dedicated to

family. Emotion flooded him. He had feelings for her. What was he going to do about that?

"It was in his blood," Liva Zook said suddenly. "Rebellion. He held on to that adornment out of pride, hiding it away and thinking no one knew about it. It took him on a dangerous path, like his grandfather before him."

He blinked. "I'm sorry?" He glanced at Eli. "I don't understand."

Eli bent toward his mother, saying something in a fast patter of the Low German the Amish used among themselves.

She shook her head, replying quickly, almost as if she argued with him. Then she stopped, closing her eyes.

It was unnerving. Had she gone to sleep in the middle of the conversation?

"What did she say?" Eli must know.

Eli shrugged, but his candid blue eyes no longer met Tyler's so forthrightly. "Old folks' gossip, *ja*. She has forgotten now. That's how it is sometimes."

There was more to it than that. His instincts told him. Eli knew perfectly well what his mother meant, but he didn't want to repeat it.

He could hardly cross-examine an elderly woman, but Eli was another story. "It was you who found him, wasn't it?"

Eli's face tightened. *"Ja,"* he said. "Heard the cows, I did, still in the barn and not milked. I looked inside, saw him."

Eli was the closest thing to an eyewitness he'd find, then. "Where was he?"

"Chust inside the door he was. I could see things

was messed up—a lamp broke, his strongbox lying there open. I went for help, but it was too late."

His mouth clamped shut with finality on the words, and for a moment he looked as grim as an Old Testament prophet. Tyler would get nothing else from him.

He thought again of what the elderly woman had said, frowning. He hadn't expected much from this visit. But what he'd heard had raised more questions than it answered.

ELEVEN

Rachel leaned against the car window to wave goodbye to Elizabeth, who stood on the porch, her cape wrapped around her, waving vigorously until the car rounded a bend and was lost to her sight.

"She's such a sweetheart." She glanced at Tyler, wondering if he'd say anything to her about what Eli's mother had told him.

The conversation had been general during supper. His manner had probably seemed perfectly natural to the others, but she knew him well enough to sense the preoccupation behind his pleasant manner.

"She certainly is. What was the piece she was talking about? Something she had to memorize?"

So apparently they were going to continue on a surface level. They turned onto the main road, and the Christmas lights seemed to blur for a moment before her eyes.

"The Christmas program in the Amish school is one of the most important events of the year for the children. The families, too. The kids practice their pieces for weeks, and the day of the program you'll see the buggies lined up for a mile."

"Do they ever invite non-Amish?"

She smiled. "As a matter of fact, we both have an invitation from Elizabeth to attend. It's the Friday before Christmas."

"If I'm still here—" He left that open-ended.

Well, of course. He probably had a wonderful celebration planned back in Baltimore. He wouldn't hang around here any longer than was necessary.

She cleared her throat. "I'm glad you had a chance to try traditional Amish food tonight. Nancy is a great cook."

"I thought if she urged me to eat one more thing, I'd burst. I hope I didn't offend her by turning down that last piece of shoofly pie."

"I expect she understood." She gestured with the plastic food container on her lap. "And she sent along a couple of pieces for a midnight snack."

"She obviously loves feeding people. She could go into business."

They were passing The Willows at the moment, and she noticed, as always, what her competition had going on. The Willows looked like a Dickens Christmas this year.

"I wonder—" The idea began to form in her mind, nebulous at first but firming up quickly.

Tyler glanced at her. "You wonder what?"

"What you said about Nancy's cooking made me think. If we could offer our guests the opportunity to have dinner in an Amish home, that might be really appealing."

"Sounds like a nice extra to pull people in. Why don't you go for it, if Nancy and her family are willing?"

"It's a bit more complicated than that." The light was on in the back room of Phil Longstreet's shop. He must be working late.

"Why complicated? Just add it to the Web site, and you're in business."

"Not complicated at my end. At theirs. Even if Nancy and Samuel are interested, they'd have to get the approval of the bishop first."

He turned into the inn's driveway, darting her a frowning look as they passed under the streetlight. "Don't the Amish have the right to decide things for themselves? Seems pretty oppressive to me."

"They wouldn't see it that way." How to explain an entire lifestyle in a few words? "The Amish way is that of humility, of not being prideful or trying to be better than their neighbors. If something comes up that is not already part of the local Amish way, then the question would be taken to the bishop, and they'd abide by his decision."

"Still seems restrictive to me." He pulled into his usual parking space. "Maybe it would have to my grandfather, too."

"Do you think that's why he left the community?"

For a moment he didn't answer. Her hand was already on the door handle when he shook his head. "No, probably not. Will you stay a while? I'd like to talk."

"Of course."

He stared through the windshield for a moment. Warmth flowed from the car heater, and the motor sound was a soft background. The windows misted, enclosing them in a private world of their own.

"Eli's mother told me a little about my grandfather. And my grandmother." His shoulders moved restlessly under his jacket. "Funny that I never really thought much about her. But if Mrs. Zook was right, she was really the key to understanding him."

"How do you mean?" She put the question softly, not wanting to disturb the connection between them.

"The way she described her—loving, warm, gentle. It sounds as if she melted his heart. When she died, he apparently turned against everyone."

"That's the last thing she would have wanted."

He shot her a glance. "That's what Mrs. Zook said, too. How did you know?"

"If she was the person you described, then his bitterness was a betrayal of everything she was." Her throat tightened. "So sad. So very sad."

"Yes." His voice sounded tight, as well. He turned toward her, very close in the confined space. "I'm not sure I like knowing this much about my family. They didn't do a good job of making each other happy, did they?"

"I'm sorry." She reached out impulsively to touch his hand, felt it turn and grasp hers warmly. "Sometimes people just make the wrong choices."

He nodded. "Speaking of choices—" He hesitated, and she sensed a moment of doubt. Then his hand gripped hers more firmly. "I didn't tell you about the strongbox that Chief Burkhalter found. Apparently, it's been shoved in a storeroom all these years."

"Did it—did it give you any ideas about what happened?" She held her breath, half afraid of the answer.

"It had apparently been broken into the night my grandfather died. The police chief at the time must have asked my mother what had been in it. I found a list inside. In her handwriting."

She smoothed her hand along his, offering wordless comfort. How hard that must have been for him, still struggling with his grief.

He cleared his throat. "Apparently he'd kept money in there, but there was no way of knowing how much. One thing she seemed sure was missing, though. It was a medal, a German military decoration. There was a pencil rubbing of it, still fairly legible after all this time. Apparently it was something of a family heirloom." He glanced at her. "Seems funny, doesn't it? I mean, the Amish are pacifists, aren't they?"

"Yes, but I suppose it could date from a time before the family became Amish. Or from a non-Amish relative. He might have kept it out of sentiment."

"Or pride. I get the feeling my grandfather really struggled with the whole humility aspect of his faith."

"That's tough for a lot of people, Amish or not."

His square jaw tightened. "There's something else. Something Eli's mother said, about him being rebellious. She said it was in his blood. Talked about him keeping some adornment, keeping it hidden."

"She may have meant the military medal, then." She wasn't sure why that seemed to bother him.

"Maybe." He tapped his hand on the steering wheel. "I could be imagining things, but I thought Eli didn't like her mentioning that. He denied knowing what she was talking about, but I wasn't convinced. He was the one who found my grandfather. Did you know that?"

"You can't imagine Eli had anything to do with your grandfather's death." Her voice sharpened in protest. "He's the most honest, peaceful person I know."

"There could be more involved than you know."

"I know that's ridiculous." Who would he suspect next?

"Maybe so." He didn't seem to react to the tartness in her tone. "In any event, the medal, whatever it means, gives me something that might be traceable. Another road to follow."

"Good. I hope you find something." She also hoped it was something that led away from her family.

"Sorry." He smiled, a little rueful. "I guess I sound obsessed. I can't help following this wherever it takes me. But I do hope—"

"I know." He was very close in the confines of the car, and she could sense the struggle in him. "I know you don't want to hurt me. I mean, us." She felt the warmth flood her cheeks. Thank goodness he wouldn't be able to see in the dim light.

"You." His hand drifted to her cheek, cradling it.

Her breath caught. She could not possibly speak. Maybe there wasn't anything to say. Because his lips lowered, met hers, and everything else slipped away in the moment.

He drew back finally. "I guess maybe we should go in. Before your grandmother wonders what we're doing out here."

It took a moment to catch her breath. To be sure her voice would come out naturally.

"I guess we should." She had to force herself to move, because if she stayed this close to him another moment, they'd just end up kissing again.

She slid out, waiting while he walked around the car to join her. The chill air sent a shiver through her, and she glanced around.

Imagination. It was imagination that put shadows within shadows, that made her feel as if inimical eyes watched from the dark.

Tyler put his arm across her shoulders. The spasm of fear vanished in the strength of his grip, and together they walked toward the house.

"It should be down just a couple of blocks on the right." Rachel leaned forward, watching as Tyler negotiated the narrow side street in Bethlehem late Wednesday afternoon. "I don't see any numbers, but I'll look for the sign."

"It's a good thing we came together. I didn't expect this much traffic. I'd never have found it alone." He touched the brake as a car jolted out into traffic from a parking space.

"Christmas in Bethlehem. It's a magnet for tourists, and the shoppers are out in full force this afternoon."

They were several blocks away from the attraction of the Moravian Museum and the Christkindlmarket, the Christmas craft mart for which Bethlehem was famous, but the small shops in this block had drawn their share of people.

"Are you sure this is the same medal?" She'd been surprised, to put it mildly, when Tyler told her that an Internet search had already turned up the medal, or one like it, in a military memorabilia shop in Bethlehem. Since she'd planned to come anyway, it made sense that they do the trip together.

"No, I'm not sure. The dealer had a blurry photo on his Web site, tough to compare with a pencil rubbing." He frowned, glancing down at the printout that was tucked into the center console. "Still, it's worth checking out—same decoration, turning up in the same general area."

She nodded, not sure how she felt about this. "If it is the medal—well, I suppose if he valued it as much as you say, he probably wouldn't have sold it. But if the medal was stolen that night, where has it been all this time?"

"Might have been in the dealer's hands for years, and he just now got around to putting it up on a Web site."

He might be overly optimistic about that. The chances of finding the object so easily seemed doubtful to her. But if it was the right medal, and if the dealer remembered who'd sold it to him—

"There it is. In the next block." She couldn't help a thread of apprehension in her voice.

Tyler flipped on the turn signal and backed

smoothly into a parking space that she wouldn't even have attempted. "Good. Let's see what we can find out."

A chilly wind cut into her as she stepped out of the car, and she wrapped her jacket tighter around her. Tyler tucked his hand warmly into the crook of her arm as they hurried down the sidewalk, passing antique shop and a craft store.

Military Memorabilia, the sign read. Joseph Whittaker, Owner. Dusty display windows revealed little of what lay inside.

"It'll probably be mostly Minnie balls and shell fragments," she warned. "There are plenty of places where a Civil War enthusiast with a metal detector can come up with those."

"Nothing ventured," Tyler murmured, and pushed open the door.

The shop was just as crowded and disorganized inside as it appeared from the street. Wooden shelves and bins held a miscellaneous accumulation of larger items, while a few glass cases contained what might have been military insignia and decoration. A Union Army uniform hung from a peg near the door, exuding an aroma of wool and mothballs.

An elderly man sat on a stool behind the counter. He unfolded himself slowly, straightening with a smile, and pulled a pair of wire-rimmed glasses from atop scanty white hair to settle them on a pointed nose.

"Welcome, welcome." He dusted off his hands as he came toward them. "What are you folks looking for today? Anything in the military line, I'm bound to have it. The best collection in the county, if I do say so myself."

"I'm looking for a military decoration you have listed on your Web site." Tyler obviously saw no reason to beat around the bush. He'd be as straightforward in this as in everything else.

"The Web site." For a moment the man looked confused. "Yes, well, my nephew did that for me. I'm afraid I'm not really up on such things. What was it you were looking for?"

She could sense Tyler's impatience as he pulled the printout from his pocket. "This medal."

The man squinted at the image for a long moment. "Ah, you collect Bavarian military memorabilia. Quite a specialty, that is. I have several pieces you might care to see."

"Just this piece." The impatience was getting a bit more pronounced. "Do you have it?"

He peered again at the sheet. "Well, yes, I'm sure I do. Let me just have a look around." He moved along behind the counter, peering down through the wavy glass and muttering to himself.

Rachel tried not to smile as he vanished around the corner of the shelves, still murmuring. "The White Rabbit," she whispered.

Tyler's frown dissolved in a surprised smile. "Exactly. I suspect he hasn't the faintest idea—"

"Ah, I know." The shopkeeper popped his head around the corner. "My nephew took some things in the back when he photographed them for the Web site. His new digital camera, you see. Just a moment while

I check." He went through a door that was hidden by what seemed to be half of a medieval suit of armor.

"If he doesn't keep track of his stock any better than that…" she began.

"…he's unlikely to know where it came from. Well, all I can do is try." Tyler drummed his fingers impatiently on the countertop.

It couldn't be this easy. That was what she wanted to say, but it hardly seemed encouraging.

The shopkeeper hustled back in, something dangling from his hand.

"Here we go. I knew I had it somewhere."

Tyler leaned forward, his face tight with concentration. The man put the medal on the glass-top counter, where it landed with a tiny clink.

Dull silver in color, the shape of a Roman cross, with something that might have been a laurel wreath design around it and a profile in the center. Tyler turned it over, frowning at some faint scratches, and then flipped it back. "What can you tell me about it?"

"Fairly rare, I assure you. Early eighteenth-century Bavarian. I'm not an expert on the period, I'm afraid. Civil War is more my area."

Minnie balls, she thought but didn't say.

"How did you come by this?" Tyler's voice sounded casual, but his fingers pressed taut against the glass.

She held her breath. Suppose he said— Well, that was impossible. Her father could not have been involved.

"Came from the collection of Stanley Albright, over at New Holland. Quite a collector, he was, but after he passed away, his widow decided to sell some things off."

"And do you know where he got it?" Tyler's gaze was intent.

The man shook his head. "I'm afraid not, but I assure you it's genuine. Albright knew his stuff, all right."

Since Mr. Albright was no longer around to be questioned, his expertise didn't help. She didn't know whether to be relieved or disappointed.

"Do you think his widow might have any records of his collection?"

"She might," he conceded. "I'm sure I have her number somewhere." He looked around, as if expecting the number to materialize in front of him. "Now about the medal—"

Rachel watched, a bit dissatisfied, as Tyler agreed to the first price that was named. He wasn't used to the routine haggling that the shopkeeper had probably looked forward to. She could have gotten it for at least fifteen percent less, but it wasn't her place to interfere.

She couldn't help commenting when they were back on the street with the medal and Mrs. Albright's phone number tucked into Tyler's pocket. "He didn't expect you to agree to the first amount he named, you know."

"Didn't he?" He looked startled for a moment, and then smiled. "No, of course not. I was just so obsessed with getting it that I didn't think."

"You're convinced this medal is the right one, then." It all seemed too easy to her. Still, the dealer's account held together. Apparently the police hadn't even tried to trace the medal at the time.

He nodded, the smile vanishing. "It's identical to

the rubbing, right down to the small chip on one of the points." He put his hand over the pocket containing the medal.

It meant something to him, that memento of the grandfather he'd barely known. Something other than a clue to the thief who'd stolen it.

She glanced at Tyler's face, his brow furrowed in concentration. Thinking about the next step, no doubt.

And where would that next step lead? If Mrs. Albright did indeed have a record of where her husband had gotten the medal, whose name would be it be?

Rachel came out of the second-floor office where she'd picked up the brochures she needed. After they'd been unable to find a parking place on Bethlehem's busy downtown streets, Tyler had dropped her off and gone in search of a lot.

At least this gave her a few moments to compose herself and think this situation through rationally. What did it say about her faith in her father, in her grandfather, that Tyler's discoveries disturbed her so much?

She was being ridiculous, letting his suspicions taint her own belief. Of course, her father, her grandfather, hadn't been involved with the theft of that medal, any more than Eli Zook had been. The very idea was preposterous.

Someone bumped into her, murmuring an apology, and she realized she was blocking traffic in the hallway. People had begun pouring from the display rooms toward the stairs. It must be a tour group, or there wouldn't be so many at once.

Clutching the awkward box firmly against her, she stepped back to let them pass, pressing against the nearest wall. She'd wait until they were gone, and then she'd go down.

She felt it then. The hair lifted on the back of her neck, as if a cold draft blew on her, but there was no draft. Someone was watching her.

She shrugged, trying to push off the feeling. She was in the middle of a crowd. Of course people looked at her as they went by, probably wondering why she was so inconsiderate as to stand there when they were trying to get down the stairs. She could hardly make an announcement, citing the awkward box she carried and the leg that was not always stable on stairs. She wouldn't if she could—she didn't care to let anyone know that.

But this wasn't just a sense of being frowned at by someone who wished she'd move. This was a return of the feeling she'd had that dark night in the sanctuary—the automatic response of the mouse that glimpses the hawk.

Turning a little, she scanned the crowd. Lots of gray heads—this was probably a seniors' tour group, come to enjoy a day of Bethlehem's Christmas celebration. A scattering of families, too—a father in a bright-red anorak carrying a toddler in a snowsuit on his shoulders, a pair of parents wrestling with a stroller and a balky preschool-age child. And a few students, laughing, jostling their neighbors even as they ignored them a bit too obviously. No one stared at her, and there wasn't a soul she knew.

But the feeling persisted, growing stronger by the moment. Then a fresh group swept around the corner, also headed for the stairs, clogging the corridor, and Rachel was carried along with it, helpless as a leaf in the current.

She struggled for a moment and then gave up and let herself be taken along. She had to meet Tyler downstairs in any event, and at least this would take her away from that feeling, whatever caused it.

Maneuvering through the crowd, trying to find something to hold on to, she reached the balcony railing just as she was pushed toward the top step. She grabbed the railing, clutching it with a sense of relief.

At least she had something to hold on to. She'd make it down the stairs all right. Goodness knew it would be impossible to fall—the packed bodies in their winter coats would certainly keep her upright no matter what she did.

An eddy in the crowd pressed her against the railing. It pushed uncomfortably into her side, sending the corner of the box poking into her ribs. She lifted the container, trying to get it out of the way, taking her hand from the railing for a moment.

The crowd lurched, for all the world like a train about to go off the track. Irrational fear pulsed through her. She hated this. She had to get out of it, get away from this feeling of helplessness.

Another, stronger push from behind her, this time doubling her over the waist-high railing. The box flew from her hands, flipping into the air and then going down, down, until it spattered on the tile floor below.

She tried to hold on to the railing, but it was round, smooth, shiny metal, sliding under her fingers. She didn't have breath to cry out. Someone shoved her again, harder, she was going to go over, she couldn't. stop herself, she'd go plummeting down to that hard tile floor, she glimpsed Tyler's startled face in the crowd below, looking up at her—

And then a strong hand grasped her arm and pulled her back. "Easy, now. Are you okay? Get a little dizzy, did you?"

A bronzed face, looking as if its owner spent most of the year on a golf course. He gripped her firmly, smiling, but with apprehension lurking in his eyes.

"Of course she got dizzy." His wife, probably, a small round dumpling of a woman with masses of white hair under a turquoise knit cap. "No wonder, with this crowd. Just take it easy, my dear, and Harold will get you down safely."

Harold was as good as his wife's word, piloting her down the rest of the stairs with a strong hand on her arm. It was a good thing, because it seemed her balance had gone over the railing with the brochures.

And then they reached the bottom, and Tyler's arms closed around her. She lost the next few minutes, hearing a jumble of concern, recommendations that she go somewhere and have a nice cup of tea, Tyler's deep voice assuring her rescuers that he'd take good care of her.

Somehow, in spite of everything that stood between them, she didn't doubt it.

* * *

Tyler held Rachel firmly as the helpful couple left, pulling her close against his side. His breathing wasn't back to normal yet, and he was torn between the desire to kiss her and a strong urge to shake her for scaring him so badly.

"Are you okay? I thought for a minute you were going to take a header all the way to the floor." He tried for a light tone, hoping to disguise the panic he'd felt in that moment when he'd seen her falling and been unable to help her.

"So did I." Her voice trembled a little, and she shook her head impatiently. "Silly to be so scared, but it's such a helpless feeling when you're losing control."

His hand tightened on her arm. "Are you hurt?"

"No, not at all." Her smile wasn't quite genuine. "But my brochures—"

"They're over here." He led her into the shadow of the soaring staircase. "About where you'd have landed if someone hadn't grabbed you."

His uneasiness intensified. Either Rachel was accident-prone, or she'd been having a surprising run of misfortune lately.

He gathered up the brochures, stuffing them back into the box, his hands not quite steady. Coincidence, that bad things seemed to be happening to Rachel since his arrival? But not entirely—her accident had occurred before they met. That didn't reassure him.

He kept a firm grip on her as they exited the building. The streets were still crowded, and a band played Christmas carols on the corner. In the glow of the streetlamp and candles from the windows, her face was pale. He read the tension there, and something jolted inside him.

"What is it?" Anxiety sharpened his tone, and he drew her into the shelter of a shop doorway. "There's something more, isn't there?"

She pressed her lips together, staring absently down the crowded street. "It… I must have imagined it." She looked up at him, the color drained from her face. "I thought someone was watching me, upstairs. And when I nearly went over the railing, it felt as if someone pushed me." She shook her head. "I must have imagined it."

The shop door opened behind him, and they had to move to let a couple come out. The irresistible aroma of cinnamon and sugar wafted out with them. The place was a bakery, with several small round tables, empty now.

"Let's get inside and have some coffee. We need to talk about this."

His heart seemed to lurch at her answering smile. The smile trembled for an instant, and her eyes darkened as if she saw right into his heart.

He cleared his throat. He couldn't give in to the urge to kiss her here and now, could he? He held the door, touching her arm to steer her inside.

For an instant she stopped, half in and half out, her eyes focused on the street beyond the plate glass.

"What is it?" He glanced in that direction, seeing nothing but the flow of traffic and the jostling crowds.

"Nothing, I guess." She shook her head, moving

past him into the shop. "I thought I saw someone staring at us. I told you my imagination worked overtime."

"Man or woman?"

"Man—youngish, wearing a dark jacket."

He paused, holding the door, scanning the street beyond. Someone had knocked him out trying to break into the farmhouse—someone had frightened Rachel with that stupid trick at the church. Maybe someone had even tampered with the Christmas lights.

Still, why would anyone care what they were doing in Bethlehem today?

He led Rachel to a table, placed the order, ending up getting hot chocolate and an assortment of cookies, and all the while his mind busied itself with the answer to that question.

Someone might well care what they were doing in Bethlehem, because they were following up on his grandfather's murder. And if someone had tried to push Rachel over that railing, it was his fault.

She wrapped her hands around the thick white mug, lifting it to sip gingerly and coming away with a feathering of cream on her lip. She looked at him, eyes wide and serious.

"I might feel better if you told me that was a ridiculous fear, and that no one could possibly have pushed me."

He captured one hand in his. "I might, but I don't like the way things are going. Someone might be worried about what we found out at the shop today. Might think we're getting too close."

She looked down at the frothy liquid. "In that case,

you'd think it would be you they'd try to push down the stairs. You're the one who's determined to learn the truth."

"Yes." That bothered him, more than he wanted to admit. "The attack on me seems pretty explainable. Thieves or vandals, hitting me so that they could get away. But you. Why would anyone want to frighten or hurt you?"

"I don't know. I'm not convinced that someone does, not really." Her brow furrowed. "Except— Well I still feel the Christmas lights could have been an accident. But someone was in the church that night." She shivered a little. "And I can't prove it, but someone did push me on the stairs."

"If so—" He felt in his pocket for the medal and pulled it out. "You'd think they'd have been better served by trying to pick my pocket if they're worried about this."

She nodded, watching as he unwrapped the medal. "Let me have a look at it."

He shoved it across the table to her, and she bent over it, studying the surface and then turning it over. Maybe the distraction was good for her. The color seemed to return to her cheeks.

She frowned, staring at the back of it. "Is this some sort of worn inscription, or is it just scratched?"

He held it up to the light, rubbing it with his finger. "I don't know. Maybe if I clean it, we'll be able to make it out." He fingered it a moment longer and then wrapped the tissue paper around it again. "If it could talk, it might give me the answers I need."

"Maybe it will anyway." She seemed to make an effort to meet his eyes. "I'll ask Grams the best way to approach Mrs. Albright. She knows everyone."

"It might be better if you and your grandmother didn't get involved in this. I don't want you put into any further danger."

"Assuming the danger is real, and not just a figment of my imagination or a series of unfortunate accidents." She shook her head. "If I went to Zach Burkhalter—well, he might take it seriously, but what could he do?"

His fingers tightened on hers. "I should move out. Not see you again. Make sure that anyone who's interested knows you have no connection with me."

"And what good would that do?" Her voice was remarkably calm. "If this incident was real, not yet another accident, then it means that the target isn't you. It's me. And I don't know why."

TWELVE

"Thank you, Mrs. Albright, but I really don't care for any more tea. Now if we could just—"

Rachel's frown didn't seem to be working, so she silenced Tyler with a light kick on the ankle. She smiled at the elderly woman across the piecrust tea table, holding out the delicate china cup.

"I'd love another cup. What a nice flavor. It's Earl Grey, I know, but it seems to have extra bergamot."

Mrs. Albright beamed as if Rachel were a favorite pupil. "That's exactly right. I get it from a little shop in Lancaster. If you think your dear grandmother would like it, I'll give you the address."

"That would be lovely." Rachel could feel Tyler seethe with impatience, and she gave him a bland smile. He didn't understand in the least how to deal with someone like Amanda Albright. He undoubtedly saw her as a contemporary of her grandmother, but she was at least ten or fifteen years older, and as delicate and fragile as a piece of the bone china on the tea table.

Elderly ladies in rural areas had their own rules of proper behavior. What Tyler didn't realize was that if he'd come alone, he'd never have gotten in the door, let alone be having tea in a parlor that was as perfect in its period detail as its mistress. Only her own vague memories of having been taken to tea with some of Grams's friends as a child had come to her rescue.

"You're running a bed-and-breakfast inn at the Unger house now, I understand. Just a nice, genteel occupation for a young girl, and I'm sure your grandmother is delighted to have you there."

Normally she'd have choked at the prospect of being called a young girl, but in this case it was best just to smile and nod. "I'm glad to be settled at home again."

Mrs. Albright nodded, eyes bright and curious as she looked from Rachel to Tyler. "And you, young man. What do you do?"

"I'm a partner in an architectural firm in Baltimore. Now about the collection—"

Rachel kicked him again. "Tyler has family ties here, though. His maternal grandparents were John and Anna Hostetler."

"Ah, of course." One could almost see the wheels turning as she ticked through the possibilities. "John had his faults, no one could deny that, but generally good, sturdy stock. Very appropriate."

Tyler had his mouth full of butter cookie at the time, and a few crumbs escaped when he sputtered in response.

Rachel set her cup down, hoping the tiny clatter masked his reaction and trying to stifle a smile of her own. She'd known what was going on from the moment they'd sat down on the petit-point chairs. Amanda Albright was sizing up Tyler's potential as a match for her dear friend Katherine's granddaughter.

Explaining that she and Tyler didn't have that kind of relationship would only confuse the issue, and Mrs. Albright probably wouldn't believe it, anyway. She had her own agenda, and nothing would deter her. It was different probably, in Tyler's brisk urban life, but in country places like this, the gossip around any young couple would include the suitability of the family lines for several generations back.

"Tyler is settling his grandfather's estate, and in the process he's located a piece that originally belonged to the family." Now that she had firmly linked their mission to the personal, it was time to broach the subject.

She nodded to Tyler. Finally recognizing his cue, he took a tissue-wrapped package from his pocket and opened it to divulge the medal.

"The dealer said that he'd purchased it from your husband's collection." He held it out for Mrs. Albright to see.

She raised the glasses that hung on a gold chain around her neck. "Yes, indeed, that was part of my Stanley's collection." She shook her head. "I didn't want to part with any of it, but my niece persuaded me to begin clearing a few of the things that don't have personal meaning to me."

"Did your husband happen to keep records of the origin of the items he acquired?" Tyler sounded as if he had faint hope of that.

"Certainly he did." She was obviously affronted that he would think otherwise.

"That was very wise of him," Rachel soothed. "So few people are as organized as he was. Do you think we might be able to find out when and from whom he purchased this medal? It was certainly help Tyler in—" she could hardly say in investigating his grandfather's death "—in understanding his family history."

"That's very proper. I wish more young people took an interest, instead of leaving genealogical research to their elders." She rose with a faint rustle of silk. "Just come into my husband's library, and we'll have a look."

Tyler had sprung to his feet as soon as she moved, and he stepped back to let her pass. Behind Mrs. Albright's back, he clasped Rachel's hand for a quick squeeze.

She retrieved her hand and followed their hostess into the next room, hoping she wasn't blushing. Well, if she was, Mrs. Albright would just think—

She stopped, struggling with the idea. Mrs. Albright would think there was something between them. She already thought that. And there was certainly something, but the chances of it leading to a real relationship were slim, maybe nonexistent.

Mrs. Albright leaned over file cabinets against the wall, peering at the labels. "Your eyes are better than mine, young man. You check for it. He organized every item in his collection and each antique in the house by type, and kept a file with its provenance."

Tyler moved with alacrity, running his finger down the file drawer labels and then pulling out one of the drawers. He paused, glancing at Mrs. Albright. "Would you like me to look through the files, or would you prefer to do it?"

She shook her head, waving her hand slightly. "You find it. I think I'll just sit down for a bit."

"Are you all right?" Rachel grasped her arm. "Would you like me to get you something?"

"No, no, I'm fine." But she let Rachel help her to the nearest chair. "This was Stanley's province, you know. I can't come in here without seeing him sitting in that chair, his nose buried in a book, his pipe on the table beside him."

Rachel patted her hand. "It must be so difficult."

"Sixty-one years, we had." She sighed. "I never thought I'd be the one to go on without him."

"I'm sorry if our coming has been difficult. Perhaps we could come another time to look for it—"

"That won't be necessary." Tyler's voice had an odd note. "I've found it." He carried a manila file folder to her.

She took it, almost afraid to look. *Please Lord. Not my father. He couldn't have, could he?*

She forced herself to scan the page. The medal was listed, with a minute description. The date Albright had purchased it. Her heart thudded. A year after John Hostetler died.

And the seller. Phillip Longstreet, of Longstreet's Antiques.

Tyler came down the stairs, suppressing the urge to take them a couple at a time. The Unger mansion, even in its incarnation as an inn, seemed to discourage that sort of thing. Nothing wrong with that, except that at the moment his muscles tensed with the need to do something—anything that would resolve this situation and lead him to the truth.

Rachel came out of the family side as he hit the hallway, almost as if she'd been listening for him. Her green eyes were anxious as they searched his face.

"Did you talk to Chief Burkhalter? What did he say?"

His jaw tightened. There was nothing, he supposed, that dictated that he had to tell Rachel. But she'd gone out of her way to help him, in spite of what must have seemed like very good reasons to tell him to get out.

Besides, he'd gotten to like the idea that he wasn't in this alone. "I talked to him." He grimaced. "He pointed out that there could be several perfectly innocent ways for Longstreet to come by that medal."

"And one guilty one." She shook her head. "I couldn't believe it when I saw his name. And I still can't, not really. He's been a fixture in the community his entire life. Surely, if there was anything to be known, someone would have talked about it by now."

"People can do a good job of keeping a secret when their lives depend on it."

She paled, as if she hadn't considered that outcome. "Your grandfather died from a heart attack, but if it was brought on by the robbery, it could be considered murder."

"Exactly." He shrugged. "I can't blame Chief Burkhalter for moving cautiously. Longstreet is well-known around here. But I've had the sense from you that he's not entirely respected."

"I certainly never meant he was dishonest. Just—maybe a bit too eager to make a good deal. If there had been rumors of anything else—well, I haven't heard them. But Zach Burkhalter would have. He knows what's going on. You can rely on him."

"He said he'd investigate."

"But you're not satisfied." She seemed to know him as well as he knew himself.

"No." His hands curled into fists. "I can't just wait around, hoping he's asking the right questions. I have to do something."

Rachel put her hand on his arm, as if she'd deter him by force, if necessary. "What?"

"See Longstreet. Get some answers myself, before he has time to make up some elaborate cover story."

Her fingers tightened. "Tyler, you can't do that. The chief would have a fit. You'd be interfering in his investigation."

"That's probably true."

"But you're going anyway." She shook her head. "Then I'm going with you."

He frowned. "I don't want to be rude, but I didn't invite you."

"I'm not going to let you confront Phil Longstreet and get yourself in trouble." Her smile flickered. "It would reflect badly on the inn if you were arrested while staying here."

"Or on you? You've been seen in my company quite a bit."

Her eyes widened and then slid away from his. "All the more reason to keep you out of trouble." Her voice wasn't quite steady.

He resisted the impulse to touch her. What was wrong with him? He couldn't pursue a romantic relationship and confront a thief at the same time.

"I'm not going to be violent. Just talk to him."

"You should still have an independent witness," she said. "I'll get my jacket. Are you going to walk over?"

He nodded, waiting while she hurried off to get a jacket. He could leave without her, but she'd just follow him. And what she said made a certain amount of sense. If Longstreet let anything slip, it would be as well to have a third party hear it.

He heard her coming, saying something firm to the dog, who probably scented a walk in the offing.

"Later," she said, pushing an inquiring muzzle back and shutting the door. She turned to him. "I'm ready."

Outside, the air was crisp and cold. It was already dusk—they'd been longer getting back from their meeting with Mrs. Albright than he'd expected. Christmas traffic, Rachel had said.

"I hope Mrs. Albright wasn't tired too much by our visit." Rachel seemed to be reading his thoughts.

"She wouldn't have needed to turn it into a tea party." A few flakes of snow touched his face, and he tilted his head back to look up. "Snow. Are they predicting much?"

"A couple of inches by morning. Good thing we went over to New Holland today." She smiled. "As far as the tea party was concerned—you have to understand that's her way. She wouldn't have talked with you at all, probably, if Grams hadn't been the intermediary."

"Something else I owe to you and your grandmother. I appreciate it." Especially since none of them knew where this investigation would lead. Would it stop at Longstreet? Somehow he doubted it.

"About Mrs. Albright—" Rachel's mind was obviously still on their encounter with the elderly woman. The Christmas lights on the window of the florist shop they were passing showed him her face in images of green and red. "She jumped to some conclusions. About us, I mean. I hope that didn't embarrass you."

"No. But you look as if it did you." The rose in her cheeks wasn't entirely from the Christmas lights.

Her gaze evaded his. "Of course not. Setting young people up in pairs is a favorite local hobby of elderly women. I didn't want you to think—well, it's ridiculous, that's all."

Without a conscious decision, his hand closed over hers. "Is it so ridiculous, Rachel?"

She looked up, and a snowflake tangled in her hair. Another brushed her cheek. "We hardly know each other." She sounded breathless.

"Timewise. But we've come a long way in a short period of time." All the more reason to be cautious, the logical part of his mind insisted, but he didn't want to listen.

"Maybe too far." It came out in a whisper that seemed to linger on the chill air.

"I don't think so." He wanted to touch the snowflakes that clustered more thickly now on her hair. Wanted to warm her cold lips with his.

But they'd reached the corner. And across the street was the antique shop, its lights spilling out onto the sidewalk that was covering quickly with snow.

He'd come here for answers, he reminded himself. Not romance. And some of the answers had to be found inside that shop.

The bell over the door jingled, announcing their arrival. Rachel could only hope that Phil would attribute her red cheeks to the temperature outside, instead of seeing the hint of something more. He was usually far too observant about the state of other people's feelings—probably part of what made him a success as a dealer.

Still, in a few minutes he'd have far more to think about than the state of her emotions. Apprehension tightened her stomach and dispelled the warmth that had flooded her at Tyler's words.

As for Tyler—a swift glance at his strong-boned face told her he'd dismissed it already. Well, that was only appropriate. They had far more serious things to deal with right now.

"Rachel. Tyler." Phil emerged from behind the counter, a smile wreathing his face. He came toward them, hands extended in welcome. "How nice this is. I was beginning to think I might as well close early. The threat of snow sends people scurrying to the grocery for bread and milk instead of to an antique shop."

"We walked over, so the snow wasn't an issue."

She brushed a damp curl back from her cheek. Maybe she shouldn't have said anything, but she could hardly avoid greeting a man she'd known for years.

"Well, what can I do for you this evening?" He rubbed his hands together. "A little Christmas shopping for your grandmother? I have some nice porcelain figures that just came in."

She glanced at Tyler, willing him to take the lead. His face was taut, giving nothing away but a certain amount of tension.

"Actually there was something I wanted to talk with you about. A piece of military memorabilia that I ran across recently."

Phil shook his head, his smile still in place. "Afraid I can't help you there. China, silver, period furniture, that's my area. You'd have to see someone who specializes in military."

He was talking too much, being too helpful. The instinctive reaction was so strong she couldn't doubt it. Phil's normal attitude with a customer who expressed interest in something he didn't have was to try to turn them to something he did.

Did Tyler realize that? Probably so.

"I already know about the object. A Bavarian military medal, early 1700s. Sound familiar?" His tone wasn't quite accusing.

Phil turned the question away with a smile. "Sorry. As I said, not my area."

It wasn't, Rachel realized. That made it all the more unusual that it had passed through his hands.

"It came from the collection of Stanley Albright,

over in New Holland. You've dealt with him, I suppose?" Tyler would not be deflected or halted. He just kept driving toward his goal.

Phil's smile finally faded. "I knew Albright, certainly. Every dealer in the area knew him. Just like every dealer knows his widow is starting to sell off some of his things. I keep up with the news, but that's too rich for my blood, I'm afraid."

He tried a laugh, but it wasn't convincing. Rachel's heart chilled. Up until this moment she'd convinced herself that there was some mistake, that Phil would explain it all away.

He'd try, she knew that much. But she wouldn't believe him.

"You didn't sell him anything?" Tyler's tone was smooth, but she sensed the steel behind it.

"No, can't say I ever had the pleasure." Phil took a casual step back, groping behind him to put his hand on a glass display case filled with a collection of ivory pillboxes.

"Odd. Because Mrs. Albright says you sold him just such a medal about twenty-two years ago."

Phil was as pale as the ivory. "That's ridiculous. I tell you I never handled anything like that. Mrs. Albright must be—what, ninety or so? She's probably mixed up. She never knew anything about his collection, anyway."

He was talking too much, giving himself away with every defensive word. Tyler should have left this to Chief Burkhalter, or at least made sure Burkhalter was around to hear this. Zach Burkhalter would know Phil was lying, just as she did.

"That might be true." Tyler's voice was deceptively soft. "The thing is, I'm not taking her word for it. If you know anything about Albright's collection, you should know he kept meticulous records. It was there—his purchase from you, a description of the medal, even the date he bought it."

Phil turned away, aimlessly touching objects on the countertop, but she saw his face before he could hide his expression. He looked ghastly.

"I suppose you know what significance this is supposed to have, but I'm sure I don't. I suppose it's possible that the odd military piece might have passed through my hands at some point in my career. I really don't remember."

"Don't you?" Tyler took a step closer, his hands clenched so tightly that the knuckles were white. "Funny, I'd think you'd remember that. The medal belonged to my grandfather. It was stolen from his house the night he died."

He'd gone too far—she knew that instantly. He couldn't be positive the medal had gone missing that particular night, even if he were morally sure of it.

Phil straightened, grasping the significance as quickly as she did. He swung around to face Tyler, his face darkening.

"I've been accused of a lot of things, but this is a first. I doubt very much that you could convince anyone, including the police, that the medal was stolen, or that it disappeared the night he died. Your grandfather could have sold it himself."

"Are you saying you got it from him?"

"No, certainly not. But he could have sold it to someone else."

"He didn't. He wouldn't. It was important to him. He wouldn't have let it go."

Phil shrugged, seemingly on surer ground now. "We just have your opinion for that, don't we? The old man was on the outs with everyone, even his own family. Who knows what he might have done? All your detective work, running from Bethlehem to New Holland—"

Before she could guess his intent, Tyler's hand shot out, stopping short of grabbing the front of Phil's expensive cashmere sweater by an inch. Phil leaned back against the showcase, losing color again.

"I didn't mention Bethlehem. How did you know we went there?" He shot a glance at Rachel, but she wasn't sure he saw her. At least, not her as a person, just a source of information. "Could he be the man you saw watching us?"

Startled, she stared at Phil, certainty coalescing. "No. Not him. But I know who it was. I knew he looked familiar. It was one of those men who were loading the truck that first time we came. The men you said worked for you, Phil."

Now Tyler did grab the sweater. "Did you send him to watch us? Did he try to push Rachel down the stairs?"

"No, no, I wouldn't. If he—if he was there, it didn't have anything to do with me."

"You were involved. You had the medal. You sold it, months after my grandfather died. I suppose you thought it would disappear into a private collection and never surface again. But it did. Now, where did you get it?"

"Tyler, don't." Her heart thudded, and she tugged at his arm. "Don't. You shouldn't—"

He wasn't listening. Neither of them were.

Phil shook his head from side to side. "I didn't. I didn't do anything. I bought it." He glanced at Rachel, a swift, sidelong gaze. "I bought it like I bought a lot of little trinkets around that time."

"Who?" She found her voice. "Who sold it to you?"

"I'm sorry, Rachel."

He actually did sound sorry. Sorry for her. Her heart clutched. She wanted to freeze the moment, to stop whatever he was going to say next. But she couldn't.

He cleared his throat, looking back at Tyler. "I bought the medal from Rachel's father."

THIRTEEN

If her head would just stop throbbing, maybe Rachel could make sense of what everyone was saying. Her mind had stopped functioning coherently at the instant Phil made that outrageous claim about her father. The next thing she knew, she was sitting in the library at the inn, Grams close beside her on the couch, clutching her hand.

Zachary Burkhalter sat across from them. The police chief should look uncomfortable with his long frame folded into that small lady's armchair, but at the moment he was too busy looking annoyed with Tyler.

Tyler. Her heart seemed to clench, and she had to force herself to look at him. He sat forward on the desk chair that had been her grandfather's, hands grasping its mahogany arms, waiting. If he was moved by the chief's comments, he wasn't showing it. He simply waited, face impassive, emotionless.

That was a separate little hurt among all the larger ones. Such a short time ago, he'd said—hinted, at least, that there was a future for them. Now, he thought her father was a murderer.

"I told you I'd investigate." Burkhalter's tone was icy. "If you'd been able to restrain yourself, we might have been able to gather some hard evidence. You can't just go around accusing respectable citizens of murder."

"*You* can't." Tyler didn't sound as if he regretted a single action. "I'm not the police. At least I got an admission from him. What hard evidence do you expect to unearth at this point?"

"Probably none, now that you've jumped in with both feet and tipped Longstreet off that he's under suspicion. If there is anything, he had a chance to get rid of it before I could get a search warrant."

"Is Phillip under arrest?" Grams's voice was a thin echo of her usual tone, and her hands, clasped in Rachel's, were icy.

Burkhalter's expression softened when he looked at her. "No. The district attorney isn't ready to charge him with anything at this point. We're looking for the man who works for him—the one you thought was following you in Bethlehem. He may shed some light. And it's possible we might trace some of the things that have been stolen recently to him."

Rachel cleared her throat, unable to remember when she'd last spoken. Shock, probably. Anger would be better than this icy numbness, and she could feel it beginning to build, deep within her.

"What does Longstreet say now?" Impossible to believe she was talking about someone she'd considered a friend, someone she'd worked with and argued with on a project that had been so important to both of them.

And all the time—all those meetings when he'd sat across from her, when they'd shared a smile at some ridiculous suggestion from Sandra, when they'd talked plans for Churchville's future—all that time he'd been hiding this.

"He sticks to his first statement. Says he bought the medal, and some other small collectible pieces, from your father shortly before he left town. Claims to have been guilty of nothing more than not inquiring too closely where the objects came from."

Tyler stirred. "He knew. He had to."

"He's confident we won't prove it at this late date." Burkhalter turned to Grams. "I don't want to distress you, Mrs. Unger, but I have to ask. Longstreet implied that some of the things he bought might have come from this house. Did you ever suspect your son-in-law of stealing from you?"

Grams's hands trembled, and Rachel's anger spurted to the surface. "Leave her alone. Can't you see how upset she is? You have no right—"

"No, Rachel." Her grandmother stiffened, back straight, head high, the way she always met a challenge. "Chief Burkhalter has his duty to do, as do I." The fine muscles around her lips tensed. "We had suspicions, that summer. Things disappeared, perhaps mislaid. A silver snuffbox, an ivory-inlaid hand mirror, a few pieces of Georgian silver. My husband thought that my daughter's husband was responsible."

"Did he accuse Hampton?" Tyler was as cold as if

he spoke of strangers. Well, they were strangers to him. Just not to her. Her heart seemed to crack.

Grams shook her head slowly. "Not at first. He wanted to, but I was afraid."

"You're never afraid," Rachel said softly. She smoothed her fingers over her grandmother's hand, the bones fragile under soft skin.

"I was afraid of losing you and your sisters." Grams's eyes shone with tears. "I was a coward. I didn't want an open breach. But we lost you anyway."

"Not at first?" Burkhalter echoed. "Did there come a time when that happened?"

"Something vanished that my husband prized—a cameo that had been his grandmother's, supposedly a gift from a descendant of William Penn. He'd intended it for one of our granddaughters. That was the last straw, as far as he was concerned. But before he could do anything, Donald was gone. Maybe he guessed Frederick was about to confront him."

"Didn't people wonder about it?" Tyler asked. "Hampton disappearing so soon after my grandfather's death?"

Burkhalter shrugged. "I've done some inquiring. As far as I can tell, Hampton came and went so much that nobody questioned his leaving at that particular time. You don't automatically suspect someone of a crime for that."

"Of course not!" The words burst out of Rachel. She couldn't listen to this any longer. "This is my father you're talking about. My father. He wouldn't do anything like that."

Grams patted her hand. Tyler said her name, and she turned on him.

"This is your fault. You're trying to make yourself feel better by blaming all this on my father." She was standing, body rigid, hands clasped, feeling as if she'd go up in flames if anyone tried to touch her. "He didn't do it. He wouldn't do anything to hurt anyone. He was gentle, and charming, and he loved his children. He loved me." She was eight again, her heart breaking, her world ripping apart. "He loved me."

She spun and raced out of the room before the sobs that choked her had a chance to rip free and expose her grief and pain to everyone.

Rachel came down the stairs from her bedroom, glancing at her watch. Nearly seven and dark already, of course, although the lights on Main Street shone cheerfully and pedestrians were out and about, probably doing Christmas shopping. The house was quiet, the insistent voices that had pushed her to the breaking point silenced now.

She rounded the corner of the stairs into the kitchen. Grams sat at the table, a cup of tea steaming in front of her, Barney curled at her feet. He spotted her first, welcoming her with a gentle woof.

Grams looked up, her blue eyes filled with concern. "Rachel, you must be hungry. I'll get some soup—"

Rachel stopped her before she could get up, dropping a kiss on her cheek. "I'll get it. It smells as if Emma left some chicken pot pie on the stove."

"She sent Levi over with it. She knows it's your favorite."

Rachel poured a ladleful into an earthenware bowl, inhaling the rich aroma of chicken mingled with the square pillows of dough that were Emma's signature touch. "That was lovely of her. Please tell me the entire neighborhood hasn't found out about our troubles so soon."

"People talk. And I'm sure quite a few heard a garbled version of the police searching Longstreet's antiques and saw the police car parked in our driveway." Grams sounded resigned to it. She'd spent her life in country places and knew how they functioned. "Did you sleep any, dear?"

Rachel sank into the chair opposite her, pushing her hair back with both hands. "A little." After she'd cried her heart out—for her father, for the trouble that would hurt everyone she loved, for what might have been with Tyler and was surely gone now. "I guess I made an exhibition of myself, didn't I?"

"Let's say it startled everyone," Grams said dryly. "Including you, I think."

She nodded and forced herself to put a spoonful into her mouth, to chew, to swallow. The warmth spread through her. Small wonder they called this comfort food.

"I thought I'd accepted it a long time ago. Maybe I never did." She met her grandmother's gaze across the table. "This business of Daddy taking things from the house—did Mother know?"

"She never admitted it if she did." She sighed, shaking her head. "That was what precipitated her taking you away. She was upset and angry over your father leaving, and Frederick—well, his patience ran out. He said, 'At least we no longer have a thief in the house.'"

She'd thought she was finished crying, but another tear slid down her cheek. "You tried to stop them from fighting. I remember that." They'd huddled at the top of the stairs, she and Andrea, listening to the battle raging below, understanding nothing except that their lives were changing forever.

"It was no good. They were both too stubborn, and things were said that neither of them would forget." She took a sip of the tea and then set the cup back in the saucer with a tiny *ching*. "I thought all that unhappiness was over and done with, and that with you and Andrea back, we could just be happy."

"I guess the past is always ready to jump out and bite you. If Tyler had never come—" That hurt too much to go on.

"Perhaps it was meant to be. I know we can't see our way clear at the moment, but God knows the way out."

The faintest smile touched her lips. "When I was little, you told me God was always there to take my hand when I was in trouble."

"He still is, Rachel. Just reach out and take it." Grams stood, carrying her cup to the sink. "I believe I'll read for a while, unless you'd like company."

Rachel shook her head. "After I finish this, I'll take Barney out for a little walk. The cold air will do us both good."

"Don't go on Crossings Road, dear. Not after dark."

"I won't." Grams couldn't help remembering her accident. "We'll take a walk down Main Street, where the shops are still open."

Grams came to pat her cheek and then headed for the steps. "Look in on me when you get back."

"I will. I love you, Grams."

"I love you, too, Rachel."

Barney trotted happily at her heels a few minutes later as she pulled jacket, hat and mittens from the closet. He knew the signs of an impending walk, even if no one said the word.

She stepped outside, the dog running immediately to investigate the snow, not content until he'd rolled over several times in it. Must be close to four inches, but it had stopped at some time since she'd come back from the antique shop. The sky above was clear now, and thick with stars.

She whistled to Barney and started down the street. Grams hadn't mentioned Tyler's whereabouts, but his car wasn't in its usual spot, so he was probably out to dinner. Or even moving out.

She tried to ignore the bruised feeling around her heart. Tyler believed her father guilty of killing his grandfather. They could never get past that in a million years, so it was better not to try.

She tilted her head back. The stars seemed incredibly close, as if she could reach out and pick a frosty handful.

Why did You bring him into my life, when it was bound to end so badly? I thought I was content with things the way they were, and now—

God is always there to take your hand. Grams's words echoed and comforted.

I don't see my way through this. Lord. I don't know how many more hard lessons there are to learn. Please, hold my hand.

Comforted. Yes, that was what she felt. She didn't see any farther, but she didn't feel alone.

Barney danced along the sidewalk, dodging shoppers—some locals that she knew, a few tourists. The Christmas lights shone cheerfully, and in every window she saw posters for the Holiday Open House Tour.

Funny. It had occupied an important place in her mind for weeks, as if its success marked her acceptance as part of this community. Now it was almost here, and she didn't feel her customary flicker of panic. There were too many more important things to worry about. The tour would go on, no matter what happened in the private lives of its organizers.

She passed Sandra and Bradley Whitmoyer's spacious Victorian, ablaze with white lights and evergreens, a lighted tree filling the front window. Across the snowy street, Longstreet's Antiques seemed to be closed, the shop dark.

Would the police have searched thoroughly? She couldn't imagine Zach Burkhalter undertaking anything without doing it well, and he'd probably love to tie recent antique thefts to Phil. But he didn't think there was enough evidence to charge Phil with anything from the past. That had been clear from his manner.

It had also been clear that he pitied her. That he

agreed with Tyler's assessment. That her father had been guilty of that terrible thing.

She stopped, staring at the shop. Barney pressed against her leg, whining a little.

Odd. The shop was dark, but she could glimpse a narrow wedge of light from the office. Phil must still be there.

If she talked to him again—just the two of them. Not Tyler. Not the police. Just two people who had been friends. Would he tell her about her father? Would he help her understand this?

She shouldn't. Chief Burkhalter had been angry enough with Tyler for his interference. He'd be furious with her if she did any such thing.

It was her father. She had a right to know. And the idea of being afraid to talk to Phil, of all people, was simply ridiculous. Snapping her fingers to Barney, she crossed the street, her boots crunching through the ruts left by passing cars.

She reached for the knob, expecting the door to be locked, but the knob turned under her hand. She'd have expected Phil to stay open tonight, like the other shops, but if he'd closed, why hadn't he locked up?

She stepped inside, reassured by the tinkle of the bell over the door and the feel of the dog, pressing close beside her.

"Phil? It's Rachel. Can I talk with you for a minute?"

No answer. The door to the office was ajar, a narrow band of light shining through it, reflecting from the glass cases.

"Phil?" she shivered in spite of the warmth of the shop, starting toward the light.

And froze at a rustle of movement somewhere in the crammed shop.

Her hand clenched Barney's collar. She felt the hair rise on the ruff of his neck, heard a low, rumbling growl start deep in his throat.

Danger, that's what he was saying. *Danger.*

She held her breath, though it was too late for that. If someone lurked in the shadows, she'd already announced herself, hadn't she?

She took a careful step toward the outside door, hand tight on Barney's collar, trying to control him. He strained against her, growling at something she couldn't see in the dark.

A step matched hers. Someone on the other side of an enormous Dutch cabinet moved when she did. Fear gripped her throat. Scream, and hope someone on the street heard before he reached her? Let Barney go?

She hesitated too long. Before she could move, a dark figure burst from behind the cabinet, arm upraised. She stumbled backward, losing her hold on the dog, she was falling, he'd be on her—

Barney lunged, snapping and snarling. Something crashed into a glass display case, shattering it, shards of glass flying. Dog and man grappled in the dark, and she fled toward the office, bolted inside, slammed and locked the door, breath coming in sobbing gasps.

Barney— But she couldn't help him. She had to call—

She turned, blinking in the light while she fumbled in her bag for her phone. And stopped.

Phil Longstreet lay on the floor between his elegant Sheraton desk and the door. His arms were outflung, hands open. Blood spread from his head, soaking into the intricate blue-and-wine design of the Oriental carpet.

Tyler wrenched the steering wheel and spun out of the snowy driveway at the inn, tension twisting his gut. He'd come back to the inn from supper to find Katherine in shock. Phil Longstreet was in the hospital, and Rachel was at the police station.

Incredible. Surely the police couldn't believe that Rachel—gentle, nurturing Rachel—could harm anyone. But he doubted that the police made their decisions based on someone's apparent character.

Think, don't just react, he admonished himself. Katherine Unger had rushed to him the instant he walked in the door. Her incoherent explanation of events had been interspersed with Emma's equally hard-to-understand pleas for her to be calm, to go and lie down, to stop exciting herself.

Finally he'd gotten both of them enough under control to get the bare facts they knew. Rachel had gone out with the dog for a short walk on Main Street. A half hour later, just when her grandmother was starting to worry, a policeman had appeared at the inn with the dog, saying that Phillip Longstreet had been injured and that Rachel was at the station, helping the police inquiry.

Emma had to restrain Katherine from rushing out into the snowy night without even a coat.

"Go after her, please, go after her." She'd grasped his arm, holding on to him as if he were a lifeline. "Someone has to be with her, to protect her. Please, Tyler. She needs you."

He clasped her hands between his. "I'll take care of her." He glanced at Emma. "And you'll take care of Mrs. Unger."

"*Ja,* I will." Emma put her own shawl around Katherine's shoulders and drew her toward the library. "Come. You come. Tyler will do it."

Now he was forced to slow down, watchful of the small group of pedestrians who hovered on the edge of the street, trying to see what was happening inside the antique shop. He passed a police car and then pulled to the curb in front of the police station, heedless of the No Parking sign.

He raced across the sidewalk, up the two steps and shoved the door open. A young patrolman looked up from the desk, telephone receiver pressed against his ear.

"Rachel Hampton. Where is she?"

"She's with the chief." He glanced toward the door to the inner office with what seemed a combination of fear and excitement. "They can't be disturbed."

"Is there an attorney with her? Because if not, I'm certainly going to disturb them."

"Now, sir—"

The door opened and Zach Burkhalter came out, closing it behind him, looking at Tyler with an annoyed glare.

"Mr. Dunn. Now, why am I not surprised that you've turned up here?"

"You're talking to Rachel Hampton. If she doesn't have an attorney with her—"

"Ms. Hampton isn't being charged with anything. And she said she doesn't want an attorney."

Tyler's eyes narrowed. "I'd like to hear that from her." Maybe it was better if he didn't look too closely at the emotions that drove him right now.

Burkhalter's annoyance seemed to fade into resignation. He opened the door. "Go ahead."

A few more steps took him into the room, and the sight of Rachel sent everything else out of his mind. She sat on a straight-backed chair in the small office, huddled into the jacket that was wrapped around her shoulders. It wasn't cold in the room, but she shivered as she looked up at him.

"Tyler." She blinked, as if she were close to tears. "Phillip…did you hear about him? About what happened?"

"Shh. It's all right." He knelt next to her chair, taking her icy hands in his and trying to warm them with his touch.

A sidelong glance told him that Burkhalter had left the door open, and there was no sound from the outer office. They'd hear anything that was said here.

"But Phillip—"

He put his hand gently across her lips. "Don't. Just tell me what the chief asked you."

The truth was that he liked Burkhalter—he judged him a good man and probably a good cop. But he *was* a cop, and that's how he thought.

"He wanted me to tell him exactly what happened."

Her eyes were wide and dark with shock. "I told him. I was out for a walk with Barney, and I saw that the office light was on at the antique shop. I thought I should talk to Phil. Just as a friend, that's all, to try and understand."

"The shop was unlocked?" His mind worked feverishly. She'd already told this to the police, so it was as well that she told him, too. He had to understand what they were dealing with.

She nodded. "I went in, calling his name. He didn't answer. And then I realized someone else was there, in the shop."

Fear jagged through him. "Did he hurt you?"

"I'm all right." But she didn't sound all right. "Barney went after him. Gave me time to run into the office and lock the door."

"Did you see his face? Who was it?"

She shook her head. "I never got a look at him. And then I saw Phil lying on the floor. His head—" She stopped, biting her lip.

He smoothed his hands over hers. "What did you do next? Did you try to help him?"

"I was afraid of making things worse. I thought I shouldn't touch the things on his desk, so I used my cell phone to call the police."

If she hadn't touched anything else in the office, that was good, but she'd undoubtedly been in there before, maybe touched things then.

Her fingers gripped his suddenly. "The paramedics wouldn't tell me anything, but it didn't look good.

They took him to the hospital. Someone must know by now how he is."

Burkhalter came back into the office on her words, as if he'd been listening. For an instant he eyed Tyler, kneeling next to Rachel, as if he weighed their feelings for each other.

Well, good luck figuring that out. He didn't know, himself. He just knew that Rachel needed help and he was going to make sure she got it.

"What about it, Chief?" He rose, standing beside Rachel, his hands on her shoulders. "The hospital must have been in touch with you."

The chief's stoic expression didn't change for a moment. Then he shrugged. "Longstreet is in serious condition with a head injury."

"Is he conscious?"

"No." He bit off the word.

That meant that the police had no idea when or if Longstreet would be able to talk to them. He tightened his grip on Rachel's shoulders. "I'm sure Ms. Hampton has already helped you as much as she can. It's time she was getting home."

"If we went over her story again, we might—"

"She's told you everything. She's exhausted and upset, and she probably should be seen by a doctor. Is she being charged with anything?"

Rachel moved at that, as if it was the first time she'd realized that she might be under suspicion. His grip warned her to be still.

Burkhalter leaned against his desk, arms crossed, looking at them. "Charged? No. But from my point of view, she quarreled with Longstreet earlier in the day. She was upset about his accusations against her father. She went to the shop."

"But I didn't—"

His grip silenced her. "She's not saying another word without an attorney present." Somehow he didn't think Burkhalter wanted to press this, not now, at least.

Burkhalter eyed him. "Actually, you had a quarrel with Longstreet today, too. And a reason to have a grudge against him."

"And I was at the Brown Bread Café having dinner this evening, which you can easily check."

The chief looked at him for a long moment, then he nodded. "You can go now, both of you. We'll talk again. Please be available."

He took Rachel's arm as she rose, but she seemed steady enough now. She looked at Burkhalter with something of defiance in her eyes.

"I won't be going anywhere, Chief Burkhalter. I have a business to run." She turned and walked steadily out of the office.

Tyler followed her through the outer office, holding the door while she went out into the street. It was dark, cold and still. The crowd had dissipated, so Rachel wouldn't have to endure their curious gazes.

"My car is right here." He piloted her to the door. "Your grandmother—"

Her knees seemed to buckle, and he caught her, folding his arms around her and holding her close. "It's okay," he murmured. "It's okay."

She shook her head, her hair brushing against his face. "I don't know what to do. Why is this happening?"

He pressed his cheek against her hair. "It's going to be all right. Don't worry."

Fine words. The trouble was, he didn't have any idea how to make them come true.

FOURTEEN

It took a gigantic effort to keep smiling when she felt that everyone who came through the door for the open house was staring at her. Rachel handed out leaflets about the history of the Unger mansion to the latest group, hoping that their curiosity was about the house, not her.

"Please enjoy your visit. If you have any questions, be sure to ask one of the guides."

A couple of her volunteer guides had, oddly enough, become unavailable today, probably as a result of last night's events. But Emma and Grams had stepped into the breach. She'd worried about letting Grams exert herself, but she'd actually begun to regain some of her zest as she talked to people about the house she loved.

And then there was Tyler. She was aware of him moving quietly through the visitors, lending a hand here, there and everywhere. They'd managed a few minutes alone to talk earlier, trying to make sense of all this.

If Phil feared that Tyler's investigations might reveal he'd bought stolen property, he might have a reason to try to stop him. But why would he have anything against her?

Everything that happened to her could have been coincidence. Accident.

Except that someone who worked for Phil had been there, in Bethlehem. And someone had attacked Phil and her.

Her head ached with trying to make sense of it. Tyler had listened to her attempts at explanation, but he hadn't offered any of his own. Because he believed her father guilty of murder? Even so, last night he hadn't hesitated to leap to her defense.

She'd been emotionally and mentally shattered, finding Phil in that state after everything else that had happened. Tyler had had every excuse to cut her adrift, even to suspect her of the attack on Phil, but he hadn't. He'd rushed to the rescue. Without him, she might well have stumbled into saying something stupid that would make Chief Burkhalter even more suspicious.

She smoothed out a wrinkle in the Star of Bethlehem quilt, trying to make herself think of something— anything—else. Christmas was only a few days away. Andrea and Cal would be back soon. She should call Caroline and urge her again to come home for Christmas. And wrapping the gifts—

It was no use. She could think of other things on the surface, but the fear and misgivings still lurked beneath. She was caught in a web of suspicion and pain, and she didn't see any way out.

The sound of the front door opening yet again had her turning to it, forcing a smile even though her face felt as if it would crack. Her expression melted into something more genuine when she saw Bradley Whitmoyer, bundled up against the cold, pulling his gloves off as he closed the door behind him.

She went forward, hand extended. "Dr. Whitmoyer, it's a nice surprise you could make it. I thought you'd be completely tied up helping Sandra with the visitors at your house."

"Bradley, remember?" The doctor managed a smile, but she thought it was as much a struggle as her own.

"It's all right," she said impulsively. "Maybe we should both agree to stop smiling before our faces break."

"That is how it feels, isn't it?" He seemed to relax slightly. "I thought I'd go mad if I heard another person say what a lovely tree we have. The only way I could get out of the house was to agree that I'd see how you're doing and report back to Sandra."

She'd take Sandra's interest as a gesture of support. That was better than assuming there was anything negative about her interest.

"As you can see, we're busy, but I think it's starting to dwindle down now. We've had a steady stream of visitors all afternoon, up and down the stairs, determined to see everything."

The fine lines of his face tightened. "I drew the line at that. Guests to our house may see the downstairs, that's all. The upstairs is strictly off-limits."

"Well, yours is a private house. We have to keep business in mind, and some of our house-tour people may be potential guests."

She was faintly surprised that he was willing to

stand here talking so long. The busy-doctor persona seemed to be in abeyance at the moment, but she suspected he'd been out early, checking on any patients in the hospital.

"Will you tell me something?" She asked the question before she could lose her nerve.

"If I can."

"Phillip Longstreet. Do you know how he's doing?"

His face seemed to close. He wouldn't answer. He'd plead professional ethics and say he couldn't. But then he shrugged.

"He's not my patient, so I don't know any details. But then, if he were, I couldn't tell you anything." His smile had a strained quality. "The police have a guard on his door, so I didn't see him, but I spoke with a resident who said he's stable. Not awake yet, but otherwise showing signs of improvement."

Something that had been tight inside her seemed to ease. *Thank You, Lord.* "I'm glad. Do you think, when he wakes up, he'll be able to identify his attacker?"

But there Bradley's cooperation halted. "I couldn't begin to guess. I understand the police think they can trace a few things stolen in the recent robberies to the shop, so it may have been some thief he was involved with." He took a step through the archway into the front parlor. "The *putz* looks very nice. Are you getting tired of explaining it to people?"

Obviously Bradley had been as indiscreet as he would let himself be. "It does get a little repetitive after a while, doesn't it?" she said. "Refreshments are set out in the breakfast room. I hope you'll go back and help yourself, although people do seem to come to a halt there."

He nodded and disappeared from view into the back parlor. She turned around, the smile still lingering on her face, and drew in a startled breath. Jeff Whitmoyer stood behind her.

He didn't seem to notice her reaction. "Sending my brother back to have something to eat? He won't. He avoids sweets, along with most everything else that makes life fun."

"I should probably follow his example. I've already been dipping into the snickerdoodles." Nerves, probably. She'd had an irresistible urge for sugar all day. "Have you taken the tour of the house yet?"

"I'll pass. No offense, but I'm not really into admiring the *decor*." He exaggerated the word. "It drives my sainted sister-in-law crazy when I refer to her eighteenth century étagère as 'that thing against the wall.'"

"I can see how it would." Both Whitmoyer brothers were unusually talkative tonight. Jeff usually only talked this long when it was a matter of a job to do.

"I heard you were the one who found Phil last night," he said abruptly.

Probably everyone who'd come through the door had heard that, but no one else had ventured to bring it up. A headache she hadn't noticed before began tightening its coils around her temples. Jeff stood there, waiting for an answer.

"That's right. I'm afraid I can't talk about it. Chief Burkhalter asked me not to say anything."

Before Jeff could pry any further, Emma bustled up to her.

"Rachel, you are needed in the kitchen, please. I will watch the door." She took the handful of brochures and gave Rachel a gentle shove.

"Thank you, Emma." She gave Jeff a vague smile and escaped with a sense of thankfulness.

Nancy Zook was in the kitchen, washing dishes, her oldest daughter standing next to her, drying.

"Nancy, you needn't do those by hand. We can use the dishwasher."

"It makes no matter. We can be quick this way." She passed a dripping plate to her daughter.

"Your mother said I was wanted?"

"Oh, *ja,* Tyler thought we should stop putting more food out."

"Tyler?"

"Here." He leaned in the doorway at the mention of his name. "According to my watch, the house tour hours are about over. But if Nancy keeps feeding those people, they're never going to leave." He nodded toward the chattering crowd clustered around the table at the far end of the breakfast room.

She glanced at Black Forest mantel clock. "It really is time." Her whole body seemed to sag in relief. "Nancy, I agree. No more food for them. Take the rest of it home for your family, all right?"

"That will be nice for our second-Christmas visitors, it will," Nancy said. "You don't worry about the kitchen. We will finish the cleanup in here."

"But—"

"Don't argue." Tyler's hand brushed hers in a gesture of support that seemed to reverberate through her entire body. "When you get a chance, I want to show you the medal." He lowered his voice, stepping back into the hallway and drawing her with him. "Those scratches on the back—there was something there. Faint, but it looks like someone scratched a triangle with something else inside it."

She tried to focus her tired brain on it. "Does that mean something?"

He shrugged. "I'm not sure. The triangle is a symbol of the Trinity, of course. Maybe my grandfather felt better about having a military decoration if he added a Christian symbol." He frowned. "It doesn't have anything to do with the robbery, but I can't help thinking about what Eli's mother said. Wondering what she really meant."

"Maybe I can talk to Emma after everything calms down." If it ever did. "She might have some insight."

"Good idea." He touched her shoulder, a feather-light brush of his fingers. "I'm going upstairs to get that last group moving. Just sit down and put your feet up for a moment."

She couldn't do that, but she appreciated the thought. "Thank you."

For a moment longer he stood motionless, his hand touching her, and then something guarded and aware came into his eyes. He turned and headed for the stairs.

Rachel swallowed hard, trying to get rid of the lump that had formed in her throat. To say nothing of the hot tears that prickled her eyes.

No matter how kind and helpful Tyler was, the events of the past still stood like a wall between them. And she was afraid they always would.

It had taken more than a few minutes, despite Tyler's best intentions, to clear the house of visitors, but finally the last of them were gone. Nancy and Emma had insisted on cleaning up the kitchen. Rachel had intended to leave some of the cleanup until tomorrow, but her helpers wouldn't hear of it.

And she had to admit they were right. Dirty dishes left in the sink, chairs pulled out of their proper places, a glass left on a tabletop—all offended her innkeeper's sense of what was right. Andrea might consider her the least-organized person in the world where record-keeping was concerned, but the house had to look right or she wouldn't sleep.

Once the Zook family had taken their leave, chattering as happily as if they'd been to a party instead of working hard for hours, she tucked Grams up in bed, Barney dozing on the rug next to her.

She went back downstairs, knowing she couldn't go to bed yet. Sleep wouldn't come, and she'd just lie in the dark and worry.

She walked into the library, where the last embers of the fire were dying in the fireplace. She sank down on the couch facing it, too tired to throw another log on. Silence set in, and with it came the fear that was becoming too familiar. And the questions.

I don't know what to think, Lord. How could the father I idolized have done these things?

One of the words she'd just used stopped her. *Idolized.* That was not a word to be used lightly, was it? Natural enough for a child to love her father, even if he hadn't been what the world would consider a good father.

But idolize? That smacked of something forbidden in her faith. Thoughts crept out of hiding, images from the past. How often had she let her feelings about her father's abandonment get between her and a relationship with someone else?

Is that really what I've been doing, Lord? I didn't mean to. I just never saw it.

Before she could pursue that uncomfortable line of thought, she heard a step. Tyler came in. One look at his face told her this endless day was not yet over. It was set in a mask, behind which she could sense something dark and implacable moving.

"We have to talk."

She steeled herself. What now? "If this is about the attack on Phillip—"

He dismissed her idea with a curt gesture of one hand. "No. Not Longstreet. You."

"Me?" Her voice came out in a squeak. "What about me?"

His jaw was hard as marble. "Showing people around the house was educational. Very. One woman in that last group especially admired the desk in the upstairs hall."

"It's a nice piece." She had to struggle to sound normal.

"Yes. And you let me believe it had been sitting

in that spot for a couple of generations. But it hasn't, has it?"

"I didn't—" The attack, coming on ground she'd totally forgotten in the sweep of other events, took her off guard.

"I told you it reminded me of one that had been in my grandfather's house. When that woman was babbling on about the style and finish, I remembered it. I remembered hiding under that desk while my grandfather and mother shouted at each other. I had a brand-new penknife that my father had given me, and I used it to carve my initials on the underside, in the corner, where no one would see. T.D. Guess what, Rachel? They're still there."

She could face this attack better on her feet. She stood, facing him. She wouldn't be a coward about it.

"I didn't know. How could I know that the desk came from your grandfather's house?"

"You knew that it hadn't been standing in the upstairs hall for a hundred years. You could have told me that."

She could have. She hadn't.

"Tyler, try to understand. I didn't know, then, what you—"

What you would come to mean to me. No, she couldn't say that. Not now.

"I didn't know whether it meant anything that it was here. I found the desk in one of the outbuildings when I was decorating the inn. You've seen those buildings—they're crammed with cast-off furniture. It was just another piece."

He wasn't buying it. "After I mentioned the similarity to my grandfather's desk, you had to have known it might be significant. You should have told me."

"And could I have trusted you not to make too much of it?" Anger and tears were both perilously near the surface. "You've been so obsessed with finding out the truth, that you haven't cared who got hurt in the process. Our having the desk could be perfectly innocent. My grandfather might have picked it up at a sale anytime."

"Or not. It could be confirmation that someone from this house was involved in my grandfather's death." He was armored against her by his anger and determination. "You didn't tell me the truth, Rachel. All along, you've only been helping me as a way of protecting your own family. Isn't that right?"

Her head was throbbing with the effort to hold back tears. "You can't believe that."

"I can't believe anything else." The words had an echo of finality about them. He turned toward the hall. "In the morning I'll look for another place to stay until all of this is settled."

He walked out, and she heard his steps mounting the central staircase. She listened, frozen, until they faded away. Then she sank back onto the sofa and buried her face in her hands.

Forgive me, Father. Please forgive me. I know that Tyler never will. I'll try to accept that. I was wrong. But I have to protect my family, don't I?

Tears spilled through her hands, dropping to her lap. *Do you?* The question formed in her heart. *Can you protect your family by hiding the truth?*

I need this, Father. The cry came from her inner-most heart. *I lost my family, and I need to bring it back together again. Isn't that the right thing to do?*

The answer was there. It had been all along, but she hadn't been willing to face it. She couldn't go back and recreate the family that she imagined they'd been once. That idealized image had probably never really existed.

And she couldn't build a future based on a lie. Her heart twisted, feeling as if it would break in two. She'd already lost Tyler, and whatever might have been between them. She couldn't go on trying to cover up, trying to pretend her way back to an imaginary family.

I've been wrong, Father. So wrong. Please, forgive me and show me what to do.

She already knew, didn't she? If her father was guilty, the truth would have to come out. And if evidence of that guilt lay anywhere in the house or grounds, she'd have to find it.

She leaned against the couch back, too tired to move. She couldn't start searching attics and cellars now. Even if she had the strength, she couldn't risk waking Grams.

In the morning. She pushed herself wearily to her feet. She'd start in the morning, assuming the police didn't decide to arrest her by then for the attack on Phil. She had the list of items that were missing from the farmhouse. If any of them were on Unger property, she'd find them, and let the truth emerge where it would.

And in the morning Tyler would leave. She rubbed

her temples. Lying awake all night worrying about it wouldn't change anything. She'd take a couple of aspirins and have a cup of the cocoa Emma had left on the stove. Maybe, somehow, she'd be able to sleep.

Tyler had been staring at the ceiling for what seemed like hours. Probably had been. He turned his head to look at the bedside clock: 4:00 a.m.—the darkest watches of the night, with dawn far away and sleep not coming. It was the hour of soul searching.

He got up, moving quietly to the window that looked out on the lane and drawing back the curtain. It was snowing again, the thickly falling drifts muffling everything. The lights in front of the inn were misty haloes, and nothing moved on the street.

Was he being unjust to Rachel? He understood, only too well, her need to protect her family. She'd been eight when she'd lost all the stability in her life. Small wonder that she was trying desperately to protect what she had left of family.

But she'd lied to him. Not overtly, but it was a lie all the same. If she'd just told him, the day he'd talked about the desk—

What would he have done? He hadn't remembered, then, about the initials. He wouldn't have been able to identify it any sooner. But if she'd been honest, they could have searched for the truth together.

That was the worst thing about it. That he'd begun to trust her, care for her, maybe even love her, and she'd been keeping secrets from him.

He moved away from the window, letting the

curtain fall. There was no point in going over it and over it. Facts were important to him, concrete facts, not emotions and wishful thinking.

The desk was certainly concrete enough. It had seemed huge to him when he was a child playing underneath it, imagining it alternately a fort and a castle. He'd needed a shelter during that visit, with his mother and grandfather constantly at each other's throats.

Giving in to the urge to look at it again, he opened his door and stepped out into the hall. No need to worry about anyone seeing him in his T-shirt and sweatpants—he was the only person in this part of the house tonight. When he moved out in the morning, it would be empty.

The thought didn't give him any satisfaction. He ran his hand along the smooth surface of the slanted desktop. Rachel had done a good job with it, as she had with everything she'd touched in preparing the inn. She'd taken infinite care. Did she even realize that she was trying to recreate the family and security she'd lost?

He stiffened, hand tightening on the edge of the desk. That sounded like the dog, over in the other wing of the house. But Barney never barked at night.

A cold breath seemed to move along his skin. The barking was more insistent. Something was wrong. Someone—Rachel or her grandmother—would have silenced the dog by now. His heart chilled. If they could.

He was running, moving beyond rational thought, knowing he had to get to Rachel. Down the stairs two at a time, stumbling once as his bare feet hit the polished floor. The dim light that Rachel always left on in the downstairs hallway—it was off.

His fear ratcheted up a notch. He grabbed the door handle, already thinking ahead to how he'd get into the east wing if it were locked, but it opened easily under his hand.

Race through the library, pitch-black, stumbling into a chair, then a lamp table. Out into the small landing at the base of the stairs. Up the second set of steps, no breath left to call out, just get there. The dog's barking changed to a long, high-pitched howl, raking his nerves with fear.

Get to the upstairs hall, and now he knew his fears were justified. Barney clawed at Rachel's door, frantically trying to get in. From the crack under the door came a blast of cold air. One of the windows must be wide-open in the room. Or the door onto Rachel's tiny balcony.

Grab the knob. Locked. He'd known it would be. No time to analyze or plan. Draw back. Shove the hysterical dog out of the way. Fling himself at the door. Pain shooting through his shoulder. Throw himself at it again, wordless prayers exploding in his mind.

The lock snapped; the door gave. He stumbled into the room. The balcony door stood open, Rachel's slender body draped over the railing, a dark figure over her, pushing—

He hurtled himself toward them, out into the night, snow in his face, grabbing for Rachel, pulling her back, fending off the blows the other man threw at him, the dog dancing around them, snarling, trying to get his teeth into the attacker. Rachel struggling feebly, trying to pull herself back. But the man was strong, Tyler's bare feet slid on the snowy balcony, he couldn't get a grip, they were going to go over—

The railing screamed, metal tearing loose, giving way. He fell to his knees, grabbing Rachel's arm, holding her even as her feet slid off the balcony. Holding her tight and safe as the other figure windmilled on the edge for an agonizing second and then went over, a long, thin scream cutting off abruptly when his body hit the patio.

He pulled Rachel against him, his arms wrapped around her. Safe. She was safe.

She pressed her face into his chest. "Who?" Her voice was fogged with whatever had been used to drug her. "Who was it?"

He leaned forward cautiously, peering down through the swirling flakes to the patio. The man lay perfectly still, sprawled on the stones, face up. The ski mask he'd worn must have ripped loose in the struggle. It was Jeff Whitmoyer.

FIFTEEN

Would this never end? Rachel sat at the kitchen table, still shivering from time to time, her hands wrapped around a hot mug of coffee. The coffee was slowly clearing her fogged mind, but it produced odd things from time to time.

"The cocoa," she said now.

Tyler seemed to know what she meant without explanation. "That's right. He drugged the cocoa Emma had left on the stove."

"Imagine the nerve of the man." Nancy topped off the mug Tyler held. She and Emma had just appeared, as they always seemed to at times of crisis, and Nancy had taken over the kitchen, apparently feeling that food was the answer to every issue. She slid a wedge of cinnamon coffeecake in front of Tyler. "Eat something. You need your strength."

Well, the police who swarmed around the place would probably eat it, if they didn't.

Emma was upstairs with Grams, refusing to leave her alone even though the paramedics had seen her and declared that she hadn't had enough of the drug to cause harm.

Tyler had dressed at some point in the nightmare hours before dawn. He wore jeans and a navy sweatshirt, his hair tousled. She'd put on her warmest sweater, but it didn't seem to be enough to banish the cold that had penetrated to her very bones when she'd been fighting for her life.

Not that she'd managed to fight very hard. "If it hadn't been for you—"

"If it hadn't been for Barney," he said quickly. "It was easy enough to drop something in the cocoa for you, but Barney had already been fed, so he had to take his chances that no one would hear the dog."

He didn't identify the person he spoke of. He didn't need to. They all knew.

The door opened, and Bradley Whitmoyer stepped inside. Usually he looked pale. Now he looked gray— as gray as a gravestone. He'd probably had to identify his brother's body.

She found her voice. "I'm so sorry."

Bradley shook his head. "I didn't come for that."

The words sounded rude, but she didn't think he'd meant them that way. He was just exhausted beyond reach of any of the conventions.

"You'd better sit down." Tyler didn't sound very happy at the prospect.

Bradley ignored the words. Maybe he didn't even hear them. "I have to tell you. I can't hold it back any longer. It will kill me if I don't speak."

She started to protest, but Tyler's hand closed over hers in warning.

"If this is something the police should hear, maybe you'd better wait until the chief comes in," he said.

"I'll tell them." He looked surprised at the comment. "But Rachel has the right to know first. And you. It was my fault, you see."

Tyler seemed to recognize the terrible strain Bradley was under. He looked at her, shaking his head slightly as if to say he didn't know what else they could do but let the man talk.

"I was home from college that summer." Bradley didn't need to say what summer. They knew. "I was desperate for money for my education, you see. I wouldn't have gotten involved with him, otherwise."

Her heart clutched. Was he going to name her father?

"Who?" Tyler's voice was tense.

"Phil Longstreet." He looked surprised that they had to ask. "He had this scheme—he would talk people, elderly farmers, mostly, into selling things, usually for a fraction of their value. While he was in the house, he would identify the really desirable items."

"And then you'd go back and steal them." Tyler finished it for him.

"We did." Bradley looked faintly surprised at the person he'd been. "I didn't…I didn't see any other way I could stay in school. I don't suppose Phil expected to get away with it for long. He was always talking about leaving here, he and Hampton both."

Her heart hurt. Oh, Daddy. Why did you have to get involved in that?

"They did all right, for a while. Then they tried it on John Hostetler." His gaze touched Tyler. "Your grandfather sold them some pieces of furniture. Then we went back when we thought the house was empty. He met us with a shotgun. He knew what we were doing. He was going to tell Phil's uncle, tell everyone—" His voice seemed to fade out for an instant. "There was a struggle. I don't know how it happened. I knocked him down. He lay there, clutching his chest. He was having a heart attack. I knew it, and I didn't help. I let him die."

His face twisted with anguish, and he seemed to struggle to control it, as though revealing his pain was asking for sympathy he didn't deserve.

"So you made it look like a robbery and you ran." Tyler didn't seem to have any sympathy to spare.

"The next day I was going to go to the police. I couldn't stand it. But I told Jeff, and he said he'd take care of everything. I couldn't ruin my future. So I kept quiet."

"My father?" She was amazed that her voice could sound so level.

"I heard he'd left town. The investigation died down. No one ever asked me anything. I went back to college, then medical school, and then I came back here to practice."

That was why, she realized. He'd come back as some sort of atonement for what he'd done, as if the lives he saved could make up for the one he'd taken.

Bradley's hands closed over the back of a chair. "I kept expecting to be exposed. Sometimes I thought it would be a relief. But years went by, and no one ever knew. And then you came back." He looked at her, eyes filled with pity. "And Jeff told me you had to be taken care of. And he told me why."

She shook her head. "I don't understand." But she knew something terrible was coming, and she couldn't get out of its way.

"It was because of what you wanted to do. You wanted to get rid of the gazebo. He couldn't let you, because if you did, they'd find your father's body, where Jeff buried it the night he killed him to keep him quiet."

It was Christmas Eve before Rachel thought she'd begun to understand everything. Andrea and Cal had rushed back from their honeymoon, and Andrea's calm good sense had helped her get through all of the things that had to be done. Even Caroline had come, all the way from New Mexico, making light of it but seeming to feel that all of the Hampton girls had to be together at a time like this.

The police had superintended the removal of the gazebo, and the family had had a quiet memorial service for their father at the church. She'd only broken down once—when the police gave her the tarnished remains of a child's gold cross on a chain that had been in her father's pocket.

The numbness that had gotten her through the past week had begun to thaw, and she wasn't quite sure what was going to take its place. She looked around the faces reflected in the lights of the Christmas tree. Grams, Andrea and Cal, Caroline.

And Tyler. With every reason for him to leave, Tyler had stayed.

"Now that Longstreet is awake and talking, it sounds as if he's blaming everyone but himself for what happened." Cal, Andrea's husband, leaned back in his chair, a cup of eggnog in one hand. "According to what I heard, he now says that your father decided to go to the police instead of leaving town, as they'd agreed. Jeff Whitmoyer had been working on the construction project, so he knew it was ready at hand. And he wasn't going to let anyone spoil the bright future he saw for his little brother."

"We don't need to talk about it now." Andrea leaning close to her new husband, reproved him gently.

"It's all right." Rachel knew Andrea was trying to protect her, as she always did. "I'm over the worst of it." She couldn't suppress a shudder. "I guess I'm just lucky Jeff didn't do a better job of it back in the spring when he ran me down. I certainly never connected that to asking him for a quote on removing the gazebo."

Grams put a hand over hers, patting it gently. "How could you? I knew the man since he was a child, and I never suspected a thing."

"You seemed to give up your plans then, and I suppose they thought they were safe." Tyler rested one hand on the mantel, maybe too edgy to sit down. "Then I came and stirred them up again."

Caro brushed dark red curls back over her shoulder. Her bright, speculative gaze went from Rachel to Tyler. "Good thing you were here the other night."

"Good thing Barney was here," Tyler said dryly. The dog, hearing his name, looked up from his nap on the hearth rug and thumped his tail.

"Longstreet won't get off scot-free," Cal said. "The police know he's been behind the recent thefts of antiques. I suppose he thought it worked so well twenty years ago that he'd start it up again, with a couple of hired thugs. He apparently got nervous when you two started nosing around and tried to dissuade you. But his efforts backfired when Jeff decided he was a liability."

"He's lucky to be alive." She remembered that pool of blood around him on the office floor.

"He may not think so after the district attorney gets through with him," Tyler said. "But he'll fight it every step of the way, unlike Whitmoyer. I understand Sandra's trying to have her husband declared mentally unfit to defend himself."

She could actually feel sorry for Bradley, in a way. He'd been trapped by what happened twenty-two years ago, and all his good works hadn't been enough to make up for that.

"So the medal really didn't have anything to do with it, except that it left a trail to Phil." She'd probably be trying to figure out all the ramifications of what happened for months, but it was starting to come a little clearer.

"Funny thing about that." Tyler set his punch cup on the mantel and pulled something out of his pocket. He walked over to put it on the coffee table where they could see it. The medal. "I had it professionally cleaned. The jeweler brought up what was on the back, and did a little detective work on it."

He turned it over. Rachel leaned forward, staring at the symbol incised on the reverse. "It looks like a triangle with an eye inside it."

"Not a triangle. A pyramid. Turns out this was a symbol used by a number of odd little groups back in the late 1600s in Germany and Switzerland. Rosicrucians, Illuminati, the Order of the Rose—apparently my grandfather's ancestor was part of one. Small wonder the Amish didn't want to talk about it. They'd consider that heresy."

"But surely your grandfather didn't believe in that."

He shrugged. "I have no way of knowing. I wouldn't think so, but—" He picked the medal up again. "Somehow I don't think I want this as a memento after all. It can go back into somebody's collection. We exposed the truth about his death. That's enough for me."

There was finality in his words. Did everyone else hear it, or was she the only one? This was over. Now he would go back to his life.

"I think that cookie tray needs to be refilled." She got up quickly, before anyone else could volunteer to do it. She needed a moment to herself.

She went through to the kitchen, and when she heard a step behind her, she knew who it was.

"Are you okay?" Tyler was close, not touching.

"I guess." Talk about something, anything, other than the fact that he's leaving. "You know, if Bradley had gone to the police right away, my father wouldn't have died. But he would still have left us." She tilted her head back, looking at him. "I'm not going to lie to myself any longer about who and what he was."

"I'm sorry." His voice was soft and deep with emotion. "Sorry he's gone, and sorry he wasn't the man you wanted him to be."

"I'm all right about it. Really. It's better to have the truth out. I can't find my happiness in recreating a past that never existed. It's the love we have for each other as a family that's important, not the mistakes our parents made." She took a breath, wishing she knew what he was thinking. "At least you fulfilled your promise to your mother."

"I found out more than she intended. Knowing something about her childhood, I understand her better. Her mother died, and then her father shut her away from the only support system she had left."

"It's sad. If he hadn't taken her out of the church, the Amish would have been family for her, no matter what he did." It was such a sad story, but at least now Tyler seemed content that he'd done what he could.

"Enough of that." His gaze seemed to warm the skin of her face. "I have a gift for you, and I'd like to give it to you without the rest of your family looking on, if that's okay."

She nodded, unable to speak. Her heart seemed to be beating faster than a hummingbird's.

Tyler took something from his pocket and dangled it in front of her. "I picked this up when I ran back to Baltimore yesterday. It belonged to my father's mother. I want you to have it. Not to replace the one your father would have given you, but because—well, just because it seemed the right gift."

She touched the delicate, old-fashioned gold cross, her heart almost too full for words. "It's beautiful. Thank you."

He fastened it around her neck, his fingers brushing

her nape gently. "My grandmother was like you—loving, nurturing, filled with goodness. If my father knew, he'd be happy I found someone to give it to."

Her eyes misted as she traced the graceful design. "I don't know what to say."

"Then let me say it." He took both her hands in his, lifting them to his lips. "I know there are a lot of questions to be answered about the future, and I'm not sure how it will all work out. I'll move as slowly as you want, but I know right now that I want to share the rest of my life with you."

He was being careful, not pressuring her, but there was no need. She wasn't afraid anymore of what the future held. She reached up to pull his face toward hers, seeing the love blossom in his eyes.

She'd come back to this house to find something she'd lost years earlier. God had given her not only that but much more besides. She didn't have to look for home any longer. She'd found it.

* * * * *

Watch for Marta Perry's next novel,
BURIED SINS,
The final story in the exciting new miniseries
The Three Sisters Inn.
Danger awaits the Hampton sisters
in quiet Amish Country.
On sale in December, 2007 from
Steeple Hill Love Inspired Suspense®.

Dear Reader,

Thank you for picking up this second story in the THREE SISTERS INN series. With this series I come back to my own beautiful rural Pennsylvania and the good, neighborly people who live here, especially that unique group, the Amish.

The Christmas traditions I've explored in this story come from a variety of sources, some from the Amish, some from the Moravians and some from my own Pennsylvania German roots on my mother's side. I hope you'll enjoy reading about them, and if you ever have a chance to visit Bethlehem, Pennsylvania, at Christmastime, you'll never forget the experience!

I hope you'll let me know how you felt about this story. I've put together a little collection of Pennsylvania Dutch recipes that I'd be happy to share with you—some from my own family, some from friends. You can write to me at Steeple Hill Books, 233 Broadway, Suite 1001, New York, NY 10279, e-mail me at marta@martaperry.com, or visit me on the Web at www.martaperry.com.

Blessings,

Marta Perry

QUESTIONS FOR DISCUSSION

1. Can you understand the need for family that drives Rachel to try to recreate the family life she remembers as a child? Have you ever thought you'd like to go back to a time when you felt cared for and secure?

2. Tyler feels driven to find the truth about his grandfather's death, even though he never had a bond with him. Do you sympathize with his need to do what he feels is the right thing?

3. Rachel has a close relationship with her older sister, but at times feels she can't live up to the standards Andrea sets. Do you have experience of the complicated relationships that can exist between sisters?

4. The struggle to expose the truth of the past is central to this story. Have you ever experienced the difficulty of learning a long-held secret that changes your view of the past? How does a person deal with that?

5. Rachel's injury gave her time to meditate on her relationship with God and develop a deeper relationship with Him. Have you ever found that God has used a difficult time to bring you closer to Him?

6. Rachel finds comfort and security through re-creating the Christmas traditions of her childhood. What particular Christmas traditions are most important to you? Why?

7. Tyler attributes everything he knows about being a Christian man to his father. Did your parents provide a solid example of Christian life to you? If not, where did you find it?

8. In the scriptural theme, we see reflected the images of God as a stronghold and a refuge for the righteous. What particular incidents in your life are brought to mind by this verse?

9. Most Old Order Amish keep their Christmas celebrations focused on the religious celebration and then on fellowship with family and friends. Have you ever longed for a simpler Christmas?

10. Have you ever felt that the busyness of Christmas preparations keep you from properly celebrating the birth of Christ? If so, how do you deal with that?